Dancing with the Devil

AND OTHER STORIES

DAVID GARNER

2QT (Publishing) Ltd

First Edition published 2019 by

2QT Limited (Publishing)
Settle, North Yorkshire BD24 9RH United Kingdom

Copyright © David Garner

By the same author - **Last Man in Paradise**

Author's website: www.davidgarner.net

The right of David Garner to be identified as the author of this work has been asserted by him in accordance with the Copyright, Designs and Patents Act 1988

All rights reserved. This book is sold subject to the condition that no part of this book is to be reproduced, in any shape or form. Or by way of trade, stored in a retrieval system or transmitted in any form or by any means, electronic, mechanical, photocopying, recording, be lent, re-sold, hired out or otherwise circulated in any form of binding or cover other than that in which it is published and without a similar condition, including this condition being imposed on the subsequent purchaser, without prior permission of the copyright holder.

Printed by Ingram Sparks

Front cover image: iStock by Getty Images
Author's photograph: Acorn Studios of Dereham

A CIP catalogue record or this book is available from the British Library

ISBN - 978-1-913071-07-3

Contents

Dancing with the Devil
page : 9

The Angel in the Dacha
page : 47

Squaring the Triangle
page : 87

The Hidden Cost
page : 123

The Taste of a Stranger
page : 159

Dedication:

To my wife, Christine

Acknowledgements:

My grateful thanks and appreciation to Catherine Cousins and her team at 2QT Publishing, particularly editor Karen Holmes, who provided unstinting encouragement and advice despite suffering my doubtful wit.

Dancing with the Devil

They sat on opposite sides of the kitchen table, husband and wife, but not enjoying each other's company. A letter lay between them on the scarred pine tabletop, two thin sheets of cheap, lined paper, a product of continuing austerity even though the war had ended six years ago. The writing was small and neat, more typical of a woman's hand.

Joan Hitcham broke the silence. 'How long have you been sitting on this?' She waved a hand at the letter.

'A day or two,' replied Jack Hitcham, unusually defensive. He scowled in irritation. 'What does it matter? Any road, I needed time to think. More to the point, what do you think about takin' the lad in for a while?'

Joan raised her hand to her chin, elbow on the table. 'I'm not thrilled, I'll tell you that for nothing. He's been in trouble, Jack; you know that as well as I do. And why isn't he working? I know they're offering to send some money for his keep but I'm not sure it will cover the cost. And we're not exactly flush, are we?' She paused for a moment. 'I feel sorry for Kitty. I know she's your sister-in-law, but why should she expect us to take her boy just because he can't get on with her new man?'

'It's not just that, and you know it. Yes, he's been in trouble but she's askin' so as the lad can 'ave a fresh start, away from bad company. She's had enough bad luck, losin' Ted in the war, for Christ's sake. Give the woman a break; it'll just be for a few months until he's called up.' He leaned forward to emphasise a new point. 'Besides, this place could use another pair of hands, enough to keep him out of trouble, any road.'

His wife relapsed into silence, considering the proposition. Although hardly middle aged, time and hard labour had imbued her pleasant face with a faint air of permanent tiredness, as though she were in need of a long, reviving holiday. To what extent Jack Hitcham contributed to this weariness was difficult to judge, but it was certainly a factor and they both knew it.

'Well, thanks to you the place certainly needs plenty of work, but who's going to be here to show him what to do? You're away driving most days and I'm working at the shop. He'd be here on his own, getting up to who knows what.'

Ignoring the dig, Jack tackled the objection. 'You're only part time at the shop and I'm not away that much. I'd make sure he knew what to do. And it would give you a bit of a break.'

'Perhaps, except for the extra cooking, washing and ironing. But then you wouldn't know about that.'

'C'mon Joanie, you'd cope well enough. And you'd be spared looking after the fruit an' veg and the chickens. It'll be a bit of a rest cure for you.' His weathered face broke into a grin as he sensed her opposition weakening.

'Don't push it, Jack. If I agree, it'll be for Kitty, not you. As for the boy, we've only seen him a handful of times in seventeen years, and the last of those he hardly spoke. Kitty admits he's been in trouble, so we don't know what we'd be letting ourselves in for. But I tell you this: any trouble from him here, and he'll be gone from this house the same day.'

Jack's grin broadened. 'He's a Hitcham, Joanie. What possible trouble could he be?'

※

Alan Hitcham dismounted from the bus, a battered ex-services suitcase trailing in his right hand. There was no one to meet him. After taking stock of the village centre for a minute or so, he realised he was unsure of the way. He asked at the post office where an inquisitive, grey-haired woman gave directions while all the time scrutinising the new arrival.

It was a bright spring day but a chilly breeze wormed its way through his thin jacket as he trudged to the edge of the village. The few pedestrians he saw observed him closely and rather covertly, a stranger in their limited world. He passed a round-towered church, which he half-remembered, and then a straggling, neglected orchard. Here he found the entrance to an unmade track leading to his uncle's smallholding. He remembered it now. Passing the burdensome suitcase to his left hand he set off again, carefully avoiding the puddles in the ruts along the way.

The orchard's straggling trees restricted his vision along the curving track, and he walked fifty yards or so before two wooden outbuildings came into view. One was a small, open-fronted barn that housed an untidy collection of agricultural equipment, rusty and little used. The other building was a long, wood-clad workshop with a rampant growth of glossy ivy covering one end.

The Hitchams' house was set back opposite the outbuildings. The brightness of the day lent the property an air of rural charm, accentuated by patches of white May-blossom in the boundary hedge beyond. But closer inspection revealed its utilitarian construction, with plain modern bricks supporting a grey, slate-tiled roof, materials entirely lacking any local connection.

The front door was half open but Alan was reluctant to walk in without announcing his presence first. In the absence of a door knocker, he tapped on the wooden door. A woman's voice told him to come in. He did as he was bidden, the restricted lobby space forcing him to hold the suitcase in front of himself with both hands.

Joan Hitcham appeared at the end of the hallway. 'Hello, you found your way all right then.' Her smile was adequate rather than effusive. 'Have you had a good journey?'

'Yes, thanks.' His voice was deeper than she remembered but it had probably broken by now. And he was taller, although still no more than average height, a slim, gangly build bordering on skinny. This was reflected in his lean face, still adolescent but with a definite trace of Hitcham present, not a feature Joan found particularly comforting.

'I'll show you your room and then we'll have a cup of tea. I expect you could do with one after the journey.'

He gave a tentative smile and nodded by way of a reply, and Joan realised he was a little apprehensive. For some reason, she found this reassuring.

❧

And so Alan began to settle in. To Joan's surprise, her husband took the lad under his wing with determined application. There was much for Alan to learn, he kept insisting. It was as if an entirely new way of life had to be learnt and lived before Alan was called up for his national service. And to see the diligence with which Jack started to instruct his nephew in country skills, it was as if he believed the lad had never seen a cow or tree before, although Middlesex was hardly the centre of London.

During his first week, Alan was shown the boundaries of the smallholding and the adjacent nine-acre field that comprised the Hitchams' land holding. The field was let to a neighbouring farmer, the rent from which helped pay the mortgage, taken out in extremis during the depression of the 1930s. Not unnaturally, Jack did not mention the precarious nature of his finances to Alan, leaving the fact that he now worked as a lorry driver to speak for itself. But that employment left little time to work the remaining five acres surrounding the house. In his enforced absence during the war, neglect had allowed the smallholding to start reverting to nature and, on his demobilisation, Jack lacked the capital to buy modern farm machinery. But he also lacked the ambition to restore the smallholding to cultivation, for it had always been an uncertain living. Receiving small but regular pay during his army service had sapped his will to return to the struggle.

With the arrival of Alan, a degree of renewed enthusiasm became apparent. The scythe, slasher, billhook and numerous other tools were taken down from their pegs and their use carefully detailed. Jack quickly passed a series of responsibilities over to his nephew, keeping his word that Joan would be relieved of some daily chores. Alan did not find the work onerous but it was physical and time consuming, after which he slept well.

If Alan found his new life congenial, it was greatly helped by one of his uncle's particular enthusiasms. Jack was an inveterate pot-hunter. Many creatures featured in the Hitchams' meals, from the conventional rabbit and pheasant to the less well-known rook and moorhen. During the nesting season few of the larger birds' eggs were safe, even plovers and jays, although Jack was now less inclined to climb trees in search of a meal. But these activities came with a caveat: when his predations strayed beyond his own land, it became poaching, also known as petty theft. Joan disapproved but had long since learnt to remain silent about such matters, since Jack took the pragmatic view that no one could own God's wild creatures. And he could be touchy if criticised.

Jack's skill became apparent to Alan during their joint excursions around the smallholding's thick boundary hedge, where his uncle's practised eye pointed out the rabbit runs and hidden bolt holes. But, thanks to Jack, rabbits were not numerous about the smallholding, and it wasn't long before Alan was led over the boundary for a 'recce', as his uncle called it. At first, they followed a public footpath leading from the church where no one could question their presence, but they soon began to stray further afield. All the while Jack pointed out likely spots for a snare or gate-net, silent and devious methods for taking nature's bounty. Alan found a powerful attraction in this conspiratorial activity; he was a natural recruit to poaching.

It was as well that Alan was warned to avoid any mention of these activities to Joan, because she remained cool to his presence. She cooked, laundered and cleaned after him but remained politely distant. Perhaps it was just natural caution, a wait-and-see attitude that stemmed from knowledge of his previous trouble with the police. That trouble, it turned out, was not too serious, a police caution rather than a prosecution. Even so, it was enough to defer complete acceptance of Alan into her household.

On Alan's part, because of Jack's monopoly, contact with his aunt was kept largely to meal times. His days were spent outside, working on a series of labour-intensive tasks set by Jack. The lengthening evenings were spent largely in Jack's company, sometimes working on more heavyweight jobs that required two pairs of hands. But they would just as often be found at the village institute having a pint or two and a game of darts or, with the autumn evenings in mind, quietly walking the footpaths and marking the prospects for future meals.

So Alan found little time to consider Joan's coolness, if he noticed it at all. But a couple of weeks after moving in, he did find occasion to notice his aunt. It was a Sunday and Joan was preparing to attend the church's morning service. Not that she was particularly religious, but it was an opportunity to socialise that she very much enjoyed. Jack never accompanied his wife to church, for which Joan was quietly grateful. It provided an excuse for her to dress up more smartly than usual and apply a modicum of make-up. The warmer weather allowed a blouse and skirt and it was while she was putting on a lightweight coat that Alan's attention was caught by her full figure straining at the cotton blouse. The image made an indelible impression on him.

In a moment of calculated mischief, she suggested that a church service wouldn't do Alan any harm. He mumbled some sort of reply, which Joan interpreted as a refusal, just as she expected. Had she been able to read his thoughts, she might have been startled at Alan's revised view of her.

☙

Alan sat in the kitchen, enjoying his mid-morning break. A dull June morning had seen him cut down a dying apple tree, strenuous work, particularly when it came to removing the roots. A cup of tea and two biscuits provided a welcome break. The cup hovered half way to his lips as something caught his eye in the paper's sports page.

'Alan!' His aunt's voice was urgent and imperative. 'Alan, quick, get the gun. There's a fox round the chicken arks.' Joan was speaking as she hurried into the kitchen. 'Hurry, or they'll be upset and won't lay for a fortnight.'

He started up from the table but with some uncertainty. 'I haven't fired the gun. I'm not sure I'll be able to hit anything.'

'Now's your chance to find out. Quick now, or he might find a way in.'

Alan darted into the living room and took the gun from

its wall-mounted pegs. He grabbed two cartridges from the mantelpiece and hurried to the back door, closely followed by his aunt. Once outside, he opened the breech and carefully slipped a cartridge into each barrel, just as he'd seen Jack do. He closed the gun and, rather nervously, pulled back the two hammers until they clicked into place, very much aware the weapon was now ready to fire. He could hear the chickens cackling in alarm.

The two chicken arks stood on some rough meadow about forty yards from the house. The upper part of their A-frames was visible above the long grass, but Alan could see no sign of the fox. Then a renewed outburst of hysterical clucking told him the animal was still there somewhere. Advancing step by cautious step, Alan grasped the gun tightly to his shoulder, his excitement at the drama overcoming his nervousness of the gun.

Thirty yards from the arks he thought he saw a movement in the undergrowth, but couldn't be sure. A few paces more and he was sure: a russet streak hurtling away from the arks towards the boundary hedge. Swinging the barrels in that direction, he pulled a trigger. He was aware of a loud bang, a sharp blow to the side of his face, and being knocked off-balance. He stumbled and fell over.

Joan came hurrying to his assistance, smiling broadly. 'Well done! You saw him off all right.'

'I don't think I got him.'

'Never mind, you gave him a good fright.' She peered at Alan's face and then laughed. 'You seem to have done more damage to yourself than the fox. There's a cut under your eye. Did you remember to pull the back trigger first?'

'I don't know. Does it matter?'

'Yes. Didn't Jack tell you? If you pull the front trigger first, both barrels go off at the same time. It's a fault with the gun.' With that, Joan dissolved into laughter. As he climbed to his feet, Alan managed a rueful grin in spite of a painful cheekbone.

'Come on, let's get you patched up. You'll look a proper soldier with your war wound on display. Perhaps they'll strike a medal for you.' She started laughing again.

Back in the kitchen, Joan attended to his injury. Alan sat at the kitchen table while she stood over him, wiping away the blood and inspecting the cut. Joan leaned in for a closer look, frowning slightly as she peered at the damage, and Alan became powerfully aware of her proximity. He could hardly fail to see her dress flopping forward only inches from his eyes, exposing a considerable amount of two white breasts divided by a deep, shadowy valley.

'The cut's stopped bleeding. It's not too bad, just broken the skin; probably best left without a plaster. Let the air get to it and it should be fine in a day or two.' Joan straightened up and stepped back, smiling broadly. 'I'll make another cup of tea; I expect the other one's cold by now. You deserve it. After all, you're my hero now.' She suddenly became more serious. 'By the way, stop calling me Aunty; it makes me feel old. I'm Joan, if you can manage to remember.'

The ice, fairly thick on her part, appeared to have been broken.

※

As Alan became more familiar with his new surroundings, he began to spread his wings. When Jack was not available he ventured out on his own, usually to the institute, the village working-men's club. Nobody questioned his age there and he could afford a couple of pints at the club prices. Through Jack, the institute also provided a circle of acquaintances, although these tended to be men considerably older than himself. Some younger men of the village did use the place but young men of Alan's age were either barred by their youth or, if slightly older, away doing their national service.

He met Norman Lidgate through Norman's sister, Bessie. She had seen Alan during his visits to the village centre, where she worked at the greengrocers. Not being backward in coming forward, Bessie thought nothing of initiating a conversation and conveying what might be described as an expression of interest. About the same age as Alan, she was a sturdy girl with rich chestnut hair that fell around her shoulders in dense swathes. It was her most attractive feature. Although her round face was not without some youthful prettiness, it was marred by a permanent knowing expression that many found disconcerting and some found insolent.

Bessie Lidgate became Alan's first friend in the village, but it was hardly the ideal acquaintanceship. The Lidgate family were not highly regarded by their peers. The father had a few previous convictions for minor theft, and many villagers believed this propensity for being light-fingered had been inherited by his son, Norman. And it was through Bessie that Alan first became acquainted with Norman, and then became his friend.

As is the way of village bush telegraphs, news of their friendship soon found its way back to Joan. Already concerned that Jack would lead his nephew astray with poaching, she found this new friendship even more worrying. Poaching was bad enough, although not considered a major offence by many in the village, but the prospect of Alan associating with the Lidgate family was a different proposition altogether. She would speak to the lad.

Joan chose one evening when Jack was away on an overnight driving job. She waited until after their evening meal before broaching the subject. 'I understand you've become friendly with the Lidgates, Norman and Bessie.'

'Yes.' Alan sounded slightly defensive, as if anticipating worse to come.

'Hmm, I see.' Joan also sounded uncertain. 'Do you know anything about the family? I mean, have you heard anything about them from other people?'

'No, I can't say I have,' said Alan, although this was not strictly true.

'It's just that the whole family have a reputation for being, you know, a bit harum scarum. They've got a bit of history, if you know what I mean?'

He did not reply, his face blank, so Joan pressed on. 'We wouldn't want to see you involved in any trouble, Alan, that's what I'm saying. You ought to have some mates, of course, we understand that. But I'm just asking you to be careful with Norman and Bessie, you know, what you get up to.'

When under any kind of scrutiny Alan had a natural tendency towards silence, so he did not reply. Uncertain whether he had taken offence, Joan was unsure how to continue.

'You seem to have settled in here all right, Alan,' she said, deciding on a change of subject. 'Your mother says so, anyway, in her last letter to Jack. And it's good that you write to her regularly, even if it's just a short note.' Joan had instigated his letter writing simply by nagging. 'It must have been a big wrench for your mother when you left home to come up here. She must have worried for you, even though we're family. She misses you, you know.'

Alan gave a barely perceptible nod but Joan could not tell whether his tight-lipped expression was a smile or a grimace, so she abandoned any thoughts of pursuing her concerns about the Lidgates. Her attention was caught by the wireless, which had been quietly playing in the background during the one-sided exchange.

'Listen to that, Alan, it's a Glenn Miller number. He was one of my favourites.' She moved swiftly to the wireless and turned up the volume. 'I love these tunes. I used to dance to them during the war. I learnt from the Americans when they were here.' She swayed to the music. 'Are you a dancer, Alan?'

He shook his head. 'No, I've never tried.'

'Then I'll have to teach you. Come over here and I'll show you some simple steps that'll keep you on the dance floor and off the lady's toes. Here, take my hand. Watch my feet, like so, and now you do the same. You'll soon get the idea.'

Except for the incident with the fox, Alan had never seen his aunt so animated. He found it disconcerting to be so close and to be instructed to place his arms around a swaying female who, unbeknown to her, had already stirred latent youthful desires. And he was allowed no respite when the tune ended; Joan went straight into successive numbers until the programme finished twenty minutes later.

'Oh, that was wonderful! Thank you, Alan. See, you've learnt something really useful today.' Her face was flushed with a mixture of exertion and pleasure. 'Look at me – fancy dancing in a pinny. That's not going to turn many heads, is it? Still, I can remember all the steps, which is good to know. And you did pretty well yourself; you just need to relax a bit more to enjoy it. A bit more practice, and you'll soon be a proper Fred Astaire.'

Joan could hardly remember when she had last danced. Jack was a hopeless partner, not least because his heart wasn't in it. He was much more at home treading the local hedgerows rather than any dance floor. Even during their courtship he had been a reluctant dancer, preferring to visit a cinema if they ventured into town. It had taken the war, and Jack's absence abroad, for Joan to fulfil her love of dancing, particularly when the Americans arrived in numbers. Through them, she was introduced to the latest trans-Atlantic dance fads: the jive, the lindy hop and the jitterbug, a heady mix of music and movement unlike anything she and her friends had ever known before. Those lovely American airforce boys, how polite and generous they had been. And how young, even to a Joan who was in her late twenties at the time. Now, dancing again with a youthful partner revived feelings she had thought lost for ever, a return, however brief, to remembered pleasures of her younger self.

It was a subtly different Joan who now listened to the wireless, more aware when music came across the airwaves. If it seemed opportune, she was pleased to show Alan ever more complicated dance steps. As his initial inhibitions slipped away, she was delighted to find he possessed a decent sense of rhythm, certainly good enough to impress a girl on the dance floor. She took pleasure in his progress and apparent enjoyment. Even the restricted kitchen dance floor, with the pine table pushed into a corner and its uneven pamment tiles, seemed to add to Joan's satisfaction, obstacles to overcome in the pursuit of enjoyment.

It was during a slow, more intimate dance that Joan noticed. As they sashayed out of a tight corner, their bodies parted slightly and she realised that Alan's right hand was enclosing her left breast. She stopped, shocked into silence, but only for a moment.

Her voice was level but strained. 'What on earth do you think you're doing?'

Alan, his face flushing scarlet, looked anywhere but at his aunt. 'I'm sorry,' he managed to mutter.

'You're sorry? Is that it?' Her voice remained controlled, her eyes never leaving his face. 'I think you'd better get back to work.'

❧

It was all Norman Lidgate's fault. How stupid he'd been to mention his dancing lessons to this so-called friend.

Ever since that fateful day, he'd been subjected to a continual stream of sexual allusions about how his aunt must be begging for it if only Alan would make the first move. After a couple of weeks, when Alan admitted he had still done nothing, Norman had started to taunt him with declarations of cowardice, while bragging what he would do in Alan's place. And now, pressured into an act of reckless stupidity, it had all gone horribly wrong, just as he had feared.

Whatever had made him think his aunt would succumb to his blundering advances? She was twice his age and endowed with all the experience that marriage and life provided. It wasn't as if he had been notably successful with girls to date, either, and he wasn't sexually experienced. Bessie had seemed to hold out some promise at first but had singularly failed to deliver. And now even she had faded into the background, Alan's novelty apparently worn thin.

More pressing, what would Joan say to his uncle? That prospect made him truly fearful for he suspected Jack possessed a considerable temper when roused, and a sexually-molested wife would certainly provide the spark. It looked as though his time at the smallholding was finished. In fact, it would probably be best if he left when he went back to the house for lunch. That way, he would avoid any possible confrontation with his uncle and any further embarrassment with Joan.

In this miserable, not to say fearful, frame of mind, Alan made his way back to the house. Joan was in the kitchen when he entered and went to wash his hands. It was she who spoke first, addressing his back at the sink.

'I won't say anything to your uncle, Alan. No real harm was done, but I don't think we'll be dancing again any time soon and that's a shame.' She could see he was still avoiding looking at her as he dried his hands. 'Come on, dinner's on the table. Let's have something to eat and talk about something else. You can tell me how the weeds are growing.'

~

If Alan's thoughts had been confused and fearful, Joan was simply vexed. She could not believe how naïve she had been. A lad on the threshold of manhood, hormones raging, how could she not have foreseen this happening? After all those wartime dancing partners, there was nothing she did not know about innuendo, outright propositions and wandering hands. How could she possibly have forgotten?

She was well aware that Alan had developed during his time with them. Gone was the thin, hungry look and pale complexion. Outdoor manual labour had provided a healthy tan and bleached-brown hair, not to mention a more muscular torso that filled out his shirts to the point where she had had to move some of the buttons. Her nephew was no longer the pallid youth of his arrival but had burgeoned into a good-looking young man. All this had registered with her, and yet she had failed to foresee the obvious. Joan sighed at her own stupidity.

To a less sensitive individual – such as Jack – the relationship between Joan and Alan seemed unchanged, but a more astute observer would have noted subtle differences. Despite attributing the blame for the dance fiasco to Norman Lidgate, Alan started spending more time in his company. It was as if he were now embarrassed to be alone with his aunt, preferring younger, more easygoing company, however dubious.

Joan also changed. She reverted to the more distant relationship they'd had when Alan first arrived, although not as marked. Nor was it deliberate, for she had developed a genuine fondness for her nephew during his stay. But the dancing incident had intervened, and she was naturally more cautious.

Nevertheless, she still took a proprietorial interest in his behaviour and, once again, it was the village grapevine that provided unsettling comment. Her part-time job in the general store gave her access to every facet of village rumour and gossip, whether fanciful or true. At first there was nothing definite, only a few disparate snatches that caught Joan's ear, but enough to cause her increasing unease. Eventually there came a snippet that she could not ignore.

Joan returned home when the shop closed in the late afternoon. Alan was busy by the wood stack, splitting firewood with leisurely, economical strokes of the axe, a favoured chore. After a brief greeting, she went indoors to start preparing the evening meal. She had started on the vegetables when Alan entered the kitchen.

'Have you had a busy day?' Joan asked.

'Yes, pretty much as usual. There were eleven eggs but one of the hens in the big ark looks a bit iffy.'

'Get Jack to have a look at it. They're really due for some new stock; old birds don't lay as well and we can't afford to carry passengers.' Joan paused, reluctant to continue. 'You were down in the village last evening, weren't you?'

'Yes.'

'Did you go to the 'Tute?'

'Yes.'

Joan sensed a certain defensiveness. 'What did you do, play darts?'

'Some of the time.'

Joan abandoned the vegetables and turned to face her nephew. 'Was Norman there?'

'No.' Alan shook his head.

'Did you stay at the 'Tute all evening?' There was no doubt it was an interrogation now.

'Yes.'

'So you didn't slip out for a walk up to the allotments or anything?'

'No, I didn't.' He wouldn't look her in the face.

'Are you sure about that, Alan?'

'Yes.'

'Don't lie to me,' shouted Joan, at the same time slapping his face with angry power. He reeled back, utterly surprised. 'Dora Claxton saw Norman Lidgate and another boy near the allotments as it began to get dark. Today I hear the allotment store was broken into last night.'

Alan made no reply, his eyes rooted to the floor. An angry red weal had appeared on the side of his face.

'I want the truth, Alan.' Joan was calmer now as she laid out her case. 'Dora didn't recognise you; she doesn't know you well enough. But I'm as sure as can be that it was you, you're that thick with the Lidgate boy. And you can't look me in the eye and deny it, which tells me all I need to know.'

Alan hadn't moved, not even to rub his stinging face.

Joan felt obliged to continue. 'At the moment nobody knows for certain it was you. But people will think the more because you're seen so often with that bloody Lidgate boy, and there's already been talk about that. But they won't be able to prove it, unless somebody else saw you for sure.' She hesitated, her face clouded with bafflement. 'You came here for a fresh start, Alan. You were doing so well, and now this.'

There was a brief hiatus when neither spoke. Despite his turned-away face, Joan could sense his tears. They weren't what she expected and they doused her anger. But there was something she needed to know. 'Did you take anything?'

'No.' At last he spoke with feeling. 'No, I didn't take a thing. It wasn't my idea, either. I didn't know what he was going to do, not 'til we got there.'

Joan took a deep breath and when she spoke her voice

had lost its harshness. 'All right, Alan, here's what you must do. You must get away from Norman Lidgate. Tell him straight that you won't have anything more to do with him. If you promise to do that, and promise to keep away from trouble in future, I'll do all I can to back you up if there's any gossip. That's the choice, Alan, otherwise I'm finished with you.'

He still could not bring himself to look at his aunt but she was insistent. 'Come on, take a deep breath, look me in the eye and promise.'

At last he raised his eyes to meet Joan's and nodded his assent.

'Promise,' she prompted.

'Yes, I promise.' His voice was quiet but not feeble.

'Good,' said Joan with an air of finality. 'Good. Now let me get on with the vegetables or Jack will give me hell for a late tea.'

※

Over the next few days Alan showed a marked reluctance to visit the village. During the day he preferred to stay on the smallholding, keeping busy as a range of early fruit and vegetables became ready for harvesting. In the evenings, which were now starting to draw in, he declined to accompany Jack to the Institute, citing a need to write to his mother or a wireless programme he'd like to hear. Joan noted this reticence but had no idea whether it was a good sign or not.

Still concerned about Alan, she was further perturbed by her husband. Late one afternoon Jack brought his lorry to the house. This was by no means unknown but it was a departure from his normal routine, where he left the lorry at the firm's yard and walked home. Now he called for Alan to give him a hand unloading several heavy sacks. Working together, they quickly shifted the load into the store room, whereupon Jack climbed back into the cab, executed a neat three-point turn and set off for the firm's yard.

That same evening Jack walked down to the village, although still unaccompanied by Alan. It was after ten when he returned, not obviously the worse for drink although Joan recognised the signs. That being so, she would normally have avoided raising a contentious subject but her concerns about Alan made her less circumspect than usual.

In the kitchen Jack helped himself to a cheese and onion supper and sat down in his battered Windsor chair. Joan came through from the living room and started washing up the cups she'd used for her and Alan's evening drink. Alan had already retired to his bedroom.

'What was that you unloaded this afternoon?' Her question sounded perfectly innocuous.

'Wheat an' laying meal, all stuff for the chickens. It'll keep 'em in tip-top condition.'

'Was it another gift from a grateful customer?'

Jack's face changed in an instant. 'What you sayin', that I've kliftied it?'

'All I know is that you turn up with sacks of this and that and we never seem to pay for them. That's what I don't understand.'

'You know nothin', woman.' Jack eyes narrowed. 'I've told you before, it's all buckshee, spare, surplus. They make mistakes when they're loadin'; it happens all the time. It's more trouble tryin' to return it, what with credit notes an' all the paperwork. It's a lot easier this way. The other drivers do the same – it's just bunce, a perk of the job. An' it's a bit handy, makin' up for a miserable wage.'

'It's still theft, Jack, and I don't like it. You could lose your job.'

'Shut it, will you? You stick to what you know an' I'll stick to mine.'

That could have been the end of the matter but, despite the warning signs, Joan felt compelled to continue. 'What sort of example is it to Alan? He was supposed to come here for a new start, to get away from trouble. You talk about poaching as if it's just some sort of harmless hobby and now you're involving him in something far worse. You shouldn't do it, Jack.'

He shifted in his chair as he became more tense. 'Fer Christ's sake, woman, what's got into you? 'E'll be none the wiser if you don't tell 'im. An' don't sit there spoutin' off at me like some Mother bloody Superior, as if you're whiter than white. I 'ave to live with tales of what you got up to in the war. That's right, give me one of your funny looks, but while I was away doin' my bit you were havin' the time of your life with the Yank airmen.'

It was an old wound re-opened and Joan was ready for it. 'Doing your bit? You went absent more times than I can count. You took a lorry without permission and got arrested in Cairo, a hundred miles from where you were supposed to be. You even went missing when the war was nearly over, hiding out in Brussels doing God knows what.'

Joan knew she ought to stop but anger made her continue. 'You were in the Service Corps, driving a lorry, just like you do now, but hardly on the front line. It was about as dangerous as my time in the Land Army. When I hear you mouthing off about your war service, I think of the boys on the war memorial like Billy Rolfe who never came back. And as for those American airmen, yes, I danced with them but after some raids the hall would be half empty, they'd lost that many. We danced, that's all, but you've always preferred to believe the worst.'

'You talk some crap,' retorted Jack, his voice rising, 'always thinkin' you're better than me, better schoolin' and the like. But you can't even 'ave kids, that's how bloody useless you are as a woman.'

A raw nerve was touched in Joan. 'That's right, Jack, it must be my fault. It couldn't possibly be you, could it, firing blanks? Jack Hitcham, a failure at something as basic as fathering a child, that could never happen.'

Instead of replying, Jack leapt out of his chair and rushed round the table. Joan raised her arms in front of her face as the first blow fell. She ducked her head and instinctively tried to make herself as small as possible even while she was seated. After a short, frenzied onslaught, Jack paused for a moment, perhaps restrained by a spasm of shame. Then he seized Joan's hair, dragging her from the chair. Both Joan and the chair fell over, the chair hitting the kitchen cupboard with a sharp crack. She gave an involuntary cry, repeated less loudly as she fell to the pamment floor. Jack seized her arms as he knelt on her, pinning her down.

'Stop.' Alan's urgent voice cut through the melee. 'Stop. You can't do that, Uncle Jack. You have to stop.' He stood in the kitchen doorway, apprehensive but determined.

Jack turned on his nephew, eyes wild, panting with exertion. In the second or so of silence, it seemed as though his anger would switch to Alan but he suddenly stood up, turned on his heels and lurched the few steps to the back door. Without looking back, he wrenched open the door at the second, furious attempt and walked outside, leaving it swinging on its hinges.

Joan was trying to rise from the floor and Alan went across to help. He shut the door, righted the fallen chair and helped her on to it.

'I'm sorry you had to see that, Alan.' Her voice was quiet, as if he were the injured party.

'Are you all right?' He didn't know what else to say.

'Oh yes, nothing too damaged.' She looked up and gave him a wan smile. 'Thanks to you. Otherwise ... well, let's leave it at that. Shall we have a cup of tea?'

Alan made the tea while Joan tidied her hair and checked for damage. There was some bruising to her arms, but they had largely absorbed the blows meant for her head.

'What will happen when he comes back?' asked Alan, concerned for them both.

'He might sleep in the barn; he's done that before. Any rate, I'll lock the bedroom door so he won't get in even if he wants to.' She smiled at him again, more certainly this time. 'It's happened before, Alan, so I know what to expect. He'll walk it off for an hour or two and then sleep on the settee if he comes in, or in the barn if not. He's got a long trip tomorrow, somewhere in Scotland, so he'll be gone early. If we work it right, we won't see him before he leaves.'

Thankful for that prospect, Alan nodded his approval. He managed to return his aunt's smile, despite being disconcerted by the intensity of her gaze.

'He'll be away for a couple of days,' Joan continued, 'so he'll have plenty of time to calm down. If he runs true to form, he won't mention tonight. I might even get some sort of present, though he won't say sorry. He never says sorry for anything.'

Alan was reluctant to ask but he wanted to know. 'Does it happen very often?'

'No, just now and then, usually when he's had a few too many and I get the devil in me. You see, I'm to blame as well. I provoked him tonight although I knew what would happen. But he made me so angry, I didn't care.' She sighed. 'I shouldn't have done it. You shouldn't have been put through that. It's not what you came here for, to see your uncle and aunt making an exhibition of themselves. It's just that I got the devil in me. You didn't know you've been dancing with devil, did you?'

Not for the first time, Alan was bemused at adult

reasoning. He could think of nothing to say.

'Don't mention it to your mother, Alan.' It was an instruction rather than a request. 'She's got enough to worry about, and it would serve no purpose except to add to the worry. Promise me you won't mention it.'

'No, I won't say anything but…' His voice tailed away.

'But what?'

'I don't know, it just doesn't seem right that…' Once again, his thoughts failed to find the right words, so Joan tried to help him.

'You're a good lad, Alan. You mean well and you're kind with it. But don't imagine adult life is all roses round the door. It's not, as you will find out, starting with when you're called up. And then, when you find the right girl and get married, you'll come across all sorts of differences that you'll have to get over. Everyone has their own difficulties; they're just part of life.'

Joan lifted her cup and drained the last of her tea. 'I think that's enough for tonight. It's bedtime.' She looked at her nephew. 'It was brave of you to help me, Alan. You took a chance there. As you saw, Jack can be spiteful when he's angry. But I'm very grateful for what you did. Like I said before, you're my very own hero.'

Joan was right in her prediction. After sleeping on the settee, Jack was gone before she rose, although she heard him leave. He left no note or message but that was of no concern to her. She cooked Alan's breakfast, but neither seemed disposed to discuss the events of the previous evening. In fact, Joan noticed Alan was rather subdued, as if still coming to terms with this new facet of his uncle's character.

When she left for the shop, Alan had already begun lifting potatoes, a slow job since they had to be cleaned of soil before being bagged up. The rows stretched into the distance and the work might have been profoundly boring but for its repetitive nature. Working on semi-automatic, Alan had ample opportunity to consider other matters. Just after four in the afternoon he stacked away his last bag of the day, had a quick wash in the kitchen and headed into the village.

When Joan returned to the house late in the afternoon, Alan was still absent. It was a little unusual but she was not at all concerned; she thought he probably needed stamps for a letter to his mother, or something similar. She had started preparing tea when he returned. He came into the kitchen through the back door and, at first, Joan did not notice. It was only when she looked him full in the face that she saw the injuries.

'My God, what's happened to you?' Joan dropped the potato peeler in the bowl and spun round to face him. She could see a long graze above his left eye, a puffy bruise on one cheek and a cut on his chin. The cut and the graze had almost stopped bleeding but blood was smeared about his face from his attempts to clean it up.

Alan spoke with some difficulty, the bruised cheek hindering articulation. 'I went and saw Norman Lidgate. I told him I wanted nothing more to do with him.'

'I see.' A look of understanding crossed Joan's face. 'It didn't go down too well, I'm guessing. No surprise there, I have to say. Come over to the sink and we'll clean you up.'

Joan carefully wiped his face, an application of antiseptic making him smart as it did its work. Despite the pain of his injuries, Alan once again became acutely aware of his aunt's proximity, disturbingly close. She gave a short, rueful laugh.

'What a pair we are, Alan, nothing but a collection of cuts and bruises.' Then she was suddenly more serious. 'I hope you managed to hit that wretched Lidgate boy.'

'I did, yes.' He sounded proud of his efforts. 'He had a bloody face by the time we stopped.'

'Good,' said Joan, with feeling. 'You did well, then, because he's a stocky boy and a bully with it, well used to scrapping by all accounts. But you're pretty solidly built yourself now, aren't you, thanks to plenty of fresh air and honest labour. And my cooking, of course.'

Alan smiled with some difficulty, pleased with Joan's compliments. She continued to fuss over him before suddenly standing back and giving her nephew a curious look. 'What made you go and see him today?'

Alan lowered his gaze to the floor and there was a lengthy pause before he spoke. 'I don't really know, but after last night it seemed the right thing to do. I wanted to get it over with.'

'I see.'

Impelled to say more, he added, 'You told me to get away from him and I have done. But it seemed like I was hiding here. After last night, I felt I had to tell him to his face, like I'd promised.'

Alan scuffed at a pamment with his foot, embarrassed by his own revelation. Joan walked round the table, sat down and studied him with disconcerting intensity.

'Well, you've done the right thing and I'm proud of you, although I'm sorry you got a bit knocked about in the process. But you kept your promise and that means a lot to me.' Joan maintained her direct gaze. 'You see, when you got tied up with the Lidgate boy I feared for you. You came here to get away from trouble at home, Alan, and he was always the sort that can get you into trouble. When my worst fears were confirmed I was … well, you can imagine.'

Joan was not yet finished and determined to pull no punches. 'You've learnt the hard way that the Lidgate boy is a thief. What you don't know is that your uncle Jack is also a thief. Oh, he hides it well; the sacks you unloaded yesterday were buckshee as he calls it, army slang for spare. But it's stealing, just the same. And from his employer, can you believe, so he could easily lose his job. But he doesn't seem to care. Something for nothing, it's just too much of a temptation for him.'

Joan had long been aware that her husband was an opportunistic petty thief. She managed to discount his poaching, for that was an activity followed by several men in the village. It was even regarded by some as a tradition, a Robin Hood view that lent an aura of romantic legitimacy to illegality. But when her husband appropriated a sack of potatoes, a bag of laying meal or fertilizer for nothing, she could find no other word for it than theft.

'I'm telling you so that you're under no illusions about your uncle. I know he's treated you well up to now and that he's fond of you. Perhaps if he'd had a son like you, he'd be different, though I have my doubts. But you've shown me you can be better than him, and that's what I want more than anything. And for your mother, too, of course.'

She reached across the table and laid her hand over his. 'You've worked hard since you came here, doing work you're not at all used to. But you've learnt and adapted, and the place looks a lot better for it. It'll be a shame when you have to go.'

Joan stopped short of saying she would miss him, although it would have been nothing less than the truth. After the turmoil of recent events, she had expended considerable time reflecting on her relationship with both Jack and Alan. Jack was quickly dismissed; nothing had changed there, except he had slipped down another notch or two in her estimation, which was already low. More difficult was her relationship with Alan. With increasing frequency, Alan reminded her of the young men she had met during the war, brief acquaintanceships among the many servicemen encountered at village hall hops or in stark military buildings temporarily converted to dance halls. When the American bomber bases started proliferating, they had provided a welcome influx of young men for the local girls, young men with every incentive to enjoy themselves, the money to indulge life and the attraction of the new.

Except not all these acquaintanceships had been that brief. With the wisdom of hindsight, it had been almost inevitable that Joan and her fellow Land Girls would meet some kindred spirits, where mutual attraction was powerfully reinforced by the pervasive tension of men at war. That was nothing more than human nature.

Now, just as that extraordinary period was receding into memory, chance had brought about circumstances that reminded Joan of those days. Different in detail, of course, but the premise was not too dissimilar: a young man shortly due for military service. And her feelings were made more powerful by his living under her roof and him being in her care. His youthful naivety had brought out her mothering instinct, which she found pleasantly surprising. But this mothering instinct was tempered by the knowledge that Alan found her sexually desirable.

The dancing incident had come as a shock, even allowing for the undiscriminating nature of rampant youthful hormones. She might have dismissed it as a momentary aberration but there was also the occasional evidence of stained bedsheets, which Joan felt obliged to acknowledge might relate to her. It was a factor she found increasingly difficult to ignore and, in a moment of self-honesty, Joan realised she was secretly rather flattered.

※

The following day was dominated by two sets of news. The first was contained in a letter to Alan from his mother: his call-up date had arrived. In five weeks' time, he was required to report to an infantry training depot in Aldershot, details enclosed. His lack of educational qualifications ruled out any hope of him joining one of the technical corps and, besides, the army was short of infantry for the emergency in Malaya and the new war in Korea.

Joan had already left for the shop when the postman called, so Alan digested this information on his own. He was quite philosophical about it; he'd known it was coming and now it had arrived. It was out of his hands but he'd choose his moment to tell Joan.

The second set of news was delivered mid-afternoon by PC Hawkes. He rode slowly up to the house on a ponderous black bicycle, carefully avoiding the deeper potholes in the unmade track. From the barn, Alan noticed his arrival with some trepidation and was haunted by the fear that some half-forgotten misdemeanour was about to catch up with him. But it seemed to be Joan he wanted to see.

When eventually PC Hawkes had remounted his bicycle and disappeared unsteadily from view, Alan walked across to the house and went around to the back door. Joan was standing in the kitchen, tiredness once again visible on her face although it had been absent in recent months.

She turned to face her nephew. 'I'm afraid it's bad news, Alan. Jack's been involved in an accident with his lorry and is in hospital in Carlisle. He's quite badly hurt by the sound of it. I'll have to phone the hospital to find out more.' She forced a grim smile, entirely without humour. 'There is more, though. They think he was drunk at the time and he could be prosecuted.'

Alan greeted this news with awkward silence, so Joan continued. 'What a carry on. How on earth am I supposed to get to Carlisle? I hardly know where it is, let alone how to get there. And Policeman Hawkes wasn't much help, either, but then he's hardly the sharpest tool in the box.

He's left me the hospital's telephone number, that's all – apart from saying Jack could be charged. I could have done without that, thank you. Lord help me, Jack Hitcham; you really are a trial.'

After this heartfelt imprecation, Joan fetched her purse from the dresser and sorted coins for the public callbox. She wasn't sure of the cost so, to be certain, Alan chipped in with some additional loose change. He also volunteered to walk with her to the telephone box in the village, for which Joan was grateful.

The call proved lengthy, requiring several extra helpings of coins before the correct ward was located and a sister found who could outline Jack's injuries. They were extensive and serious, for Jack had apparently run off the road and hit a tree. Apart from broken bones there were probably internal injuries, the extent of which had not yet been fully diagnosed. In addition, head injuries had rendered Jack barely conscious and unable to speak. In view of the distance and difficulty of travelling there, the sister advised Joan to check on Jack's progress by phone each day before committing to visit.

When the telephone call was over, Joan sent Alan back to the house while she walked the quarter of a mile to Walcott Transport's yard. Brian Walcott was still in the office hut, although it was now after five. He was a thin, undemonstrative man who spoke as though each word was costing him money. His manner towards Joan was polite but cool. He wished Jack well, of course, but there were likely to be repercussions as a result of the accident. He asked whether Joan could cope, which she thought alluded to money. Being independent minded, she said she would manage. That was the extent of the conversation, but its coolness and brevity hardly boded well for Jack's future employment.

It took until the evening before Joan felt able to talk to

Alan. She called him down from his room and they sat at the kitchen table for their nightcap. At first neither was inclined to speak and silence ensued until Joan thought it necessary to explain the situation.

'The hospital said best to wait until Jack's recovered a bit before I go up there. I don't mind admitting that's a blessing at the moment, otherwise I might murder the man. I'll wait until they tell me he's able to speak and understand what's said to him. When that happens, I'll be away for a couple of days, what with the travelling. And I'll have to stay overnight somewhere as well. But you'll be all right on your own, won't you?'

'Yes, I'll be fine.' He hesitated before adding, 'Unless you'd like me to come with you.'

'Oh no, that won't be necessary. But thank you, Alan; it's very kind of you to offer. But somebody's got to look after this place while I'm away, and you're just the man.' She managed a ruminative smile before adding, 'I suppose I'm partly to blame for this beggar's mess. He's done it before, you see. We have an argument and he goes off in a huff and drinks himself stupid. Only he doesn't usually get as far as Carlisle.'

Embarrassed by this further revelation of marital discord, Alan could think of nothing to say. Joan returned to her own thoughts, so the kitchen fell silent except for the faint tick of the wall clock. A minute or two elapsed before Alan remembered his own news. 'I had a letter from Mum today,' he began, rather uncertainly. 'My call-up has come through.'

'I see.' Joan studied Alan's face for a moment and then diverted her eyes to a mid-point somewhere above the dresser. 'It never rains but it pours, does it?' Her gaze returned to her nephew and she managed a wryly affectionate smile. 'Well, we've known it was coming. And it'll make a man of you, being a soldier. I can just see you in uniform. Very smart you'll be, and a credit to your parents. When do you think you should go back to your mother's?'

'Not yet.' He sounded unusually certain. 'I've got until the beginning of October before I have to report. I think I'll go back to Mum's a week before then.'

'Well, if you're happy with that, I'll be very grateful for your help ... and your company.' Joan suddenly felt tearful but managed to ward it off. She would not indulge self-pity. 'Are you looking forward to the army?'

'Not really, but everyone has to go so I just want to get on with it. I know a couple of others who've been called up and they seem to have managed. I expect I'll be all right.'

'I know you will, Alan, you'll be fine. Just try and keep away from those wars, will you? For your mother's sake.'

He nodded, sensing Joan's concern. But they both understood he would have not the slightest say in the matter.

❧

Alan was in bed and nearly asleep when he heard the door open. A faint light from the landing silhouetted a figure in the doorway, recognisably Joan even though she had brushed out her hair. She left the door slightly ajar; a feeble light barely illuminated a pine chest at the end of the bed. The rest of the room remained in deep, shadowy darkness.

Joan carefully felt her way to the bed and sat on the edge. 'I don't feel much like sleep, Alan. My mind's all in a whirl. I'd just like to talk for a while, if you don't mind.'

He was suddenly very much awake. Joan had never before entered his room when he was in bed. 'No, I don't mind.' His voice sounded unusually husky.

'It's strange; I can talk to you better than I can to Jack. But then he was never great at conversation. He'd much sooner be off up the hedgerows after a pheasant. You don't need much conversation out there.' Joan's voice was soft and mellow, as though she had found an inner calm after the stresses of the day. 'He had his good points when I first knew him. He must have done, otherwise we wouldn't have got married, would we? But, Lord above, now I sometimes struggle to remember what they are. And I find it hard to feel much sympathy for him, however much he's hurt. I'm more sorry for myself, which isn't very Christian, is it? But there you are; that's how I feel.'

It was like a soliloquy, for Alan felt unable to comment on such personal observations even if he had a view. But he listened, powerfully aware of Joan perched on the edge of the bed, hands folded primly in her lap.

'When you find the right girl, Alan, I hope you'll treat her well. I'm sure you will. You don't have that hardness that Jack has. Where Jack has a mean streak, you seem to have a kind one. I hope you don't lose it. There's no reason why you should.'

She was silent for a while, visible to Alan only as a dark, shadowy figure. He could just hear her soft breathing.

'Will you write to me to let me know how you're getting on? A letter would be lovely. Or you could even come and visit when you're on leave; that would be better still. Will you promise to do that?'

He gave an invisible nod in the darkness. 'Yes, I'd like to.'

'Good, I'll look forward to that.' When Joan continued, she sounded wistful. 'We get on well, don't we? Mind you, I wasn't sure at first, but you've grown on me, a bit like those weeds in the potato patch.' She laughed softly at this feeble humour. 'I don't seem to make many jokes now, not even bad ones. But we've had a laugh or two, listening to the wireless. And I've taught you to dance. I really enjoyed that.'

There was a brief silence before she added, 'Here, give me your hand.' Alan did as he was told and Joan took it in both of hers. She held it for a moment then pressed it gently to her breast before leaning down and kissing him full on the mouth. Pinned to the bed under the weight of her body, and overwhelmed by an intoxicating female scent, Alan was astounded at the things his aunt started to do with her tongue. With her thick hair freed from pins and clips now flowing sensuously over his face, he felt as if he were falling into some swirling, benign vortex against which he was utterly powerless. Intoxicated, he was a willing partner as she pulled back the bedclothes to join him in the bed.

☙

Army life suits some people and, with some caveats, it suited Alan Hitcham. His time at the smallholding had developed his strength and stamina so that the physical demands were met quite easily. And friendships developed with other conscripts, forged in their joint suffering meted out by the training staff. During his first couple of months at Aldershot he wrote two letters to Joan, but he was not a natural correspondent and the content was bland and short. She replied just once, a lengthy letter detailing various happenings around the smallholding, not least how the chickens were faring in his absence. A single line near the end said Jack was still not well enough to return home. It was signed 'from your loving aunt, Joan', and she had added two crossed kisses after her name.

Shortly afterwards he learnt from his mother that Jack had died, his internal injuries eventually proving fatal. He was to be buried in the churchyard close to the smallholding, a fitting place for a man who had derived such pleasure from the fields and byways surrounding the church. Alan tried to write to Joan but, after several attempts, failed. His condolences were conveyed by his mother.

It was a couple of months later, shortly before he embarked on the troopship, that a letter from his mother told him of Joan's pregnancy. The smallholding was being sold and Joan intended to move back nearer her home town. She was receiving help from a friend, a widower from her church circle about whom she wrote very fondly. His mother seemed curiously restrained at the news, but Alan carried this letter in his kit for many months, even after the damp, foetid heat of the Malayan jungle had reduced it to something close to pulp.

The Angel in the Dacha

THE LORRY GAVE a sickening lurch as the sandy track subsided beneath it. Mohr was half thrown onto the driver, who began wrestling the vehicle through the soft patch, the engine roaring under the strain. Thirty metres ahead, the machine gunner in the motorcycle sidecar glanced back to check the convoy's progress.

As the lorry pulled through the soft sand, Mohr tried to compose himself. Renewing his grip on the machine pistol, he resumed his vigil. How long had he been staring at the forest edge? What exactly was he looking for? 'Beware an ambush' had been the warning but he very much doubted he would spot one, not among the dense cover afforded by the endless forest. Mines were another concern and he went cold at the thought, only marginally comforted by the fact that the motorcycle combination was leading the way.

'How much further?' He sounded weary, even to himself.

'Not far now, Herr Leutnant. About fifteen minutes.'

Mohr did not reply, his mind already on other things. How could they call this a road? Were they still in Poland or was this Russia? Why was it so hot? Above all, what had he done to deserve this damnable posting? It really had been very pleasant in France.

The rough road made a junction with a railway line

and for some minutes they drove parallel to it. The forest became more broken, with some cultivated fields in the gaps. At last a hamlet came into view on the opposite side of the railway line. Mohr studied the scattered properties with disdain, a trainee architect's view of the wood-built, single-storey buildings. Hovels might be a better description, he thought. Despite being beside the rail line, the hamlet had no station that he could see, or even a stopping place for a train.

Just beyond the hamlet the little convoy, just two lorries and the motorcycle combination, crossed the railway track and came to a halt beside a low barn. But this barn had been fortified into a substantial blockhouse and was now ringed with layers of stacked sandbags and timber bastions, between which were a number of small, dark firing slits. Mohr could see a dozen or so men scattered about, some stripped to the waist as they worked. A lone sentry occupied a lookout post on top of the blockhouse.

With the convoy halted and the tension of the journey temporarily relieved, Mohr heard the inevitable derisive banter begin between the blockhouse troops and the convoy guards. He climbed down from the cab and called to the nearest soldier, 'I have to report to Major Weimann.' The shirtless figure gave Mohr a quick glance then stiffened to attention on seeing his rank. Before he could speak, a short, stocky corporal appeared from behind the lorry.

'This way, Herr Leutnant. Major Weimann is in the dacha.' He turned to the shirtless soldier. 'Find the leutnant's kit and take it to his quarters. Take the leutnant's weapon too, but unload it before you shoot someone by accident.'

The corporal set off at a brisk pace, Mohr following. Ahead was a timber house, notable for its two storeys, albeit the upper rooms were squeezed into the steep roof space. A dacha, he thought, but who would want a country home in such a God-forsaken place? The door was on the far side of the building, south facing and set back on a wooden veranda. Despite considerable sandbag protection, it did not strike him as a very military post.

The corporal halted beside the door and turned to Mohr. 'Major Weimann's office is on the right, sir.' Apparently not keen to appear before his commanding officer, he seemed to assume Mohr would introduce himself; he turned sharply about and set off back to the blockhouse.

Feeling somewhat abandoned, Mohr entered the dacha. Peering into the shadowy light, he made out a table and chairs, a sofa and, beyond that, a kneehole desk tucked into one corner. Seated at the desk was a hatless officer.

Mohr advanced smartly to the desk, halted at attention and saluted. 'Heil Hitler.'

Major Weimann looked up. 'Yes, indeed; heil our glorious Führer.' He looked about forty years old, with a stiffly handsome face on which Mohr thought a monocle would not have looked out of place. His superior, penetrating gaze contained more than a hint of the Juncker class; perhaps there was a 'von' missing from the name.

Mohr retrieved his papers from inside his jacket and placed them on the desk. Weimann opened the envelope and studied the documents.

'Well, Mohr, I see you were a transport officer but that you've done an infantry conversion course. I can't imagine you volunteered.'

'No, Herr Major, but I understand the army's needs.'

'Quite so.' Weimann continued his perusal. 'Most of your service was in France, I see; you'll find it a bit different out here. But you've been wounded. Tell me about that.'

'Our vehicle ran into a terrorist road block and went off the road. I fractured my arm and damaged my right knee.'

'Were you on an operation?'

Mohr hesitated before answering. 'No, Herr Major. We were returning from a night out.'

'Was it an ambush? Were you fired on?'

'No, Herr Major. The road block was believed to have been laid by some local youths.'

'Mmm,' said Weimann doubtfully. 'I think you'll find the terrorists out here rather more determined to kill you. But you'll find out soon enough.' He leaned back in his chair and studied Mohr carefully, as if assessing his suitability. 'What age are you?'

'Twenty-three, sir.'

Weimann nodded. 'It's a good age for a soldier. You'll have opportunities to prove your worth here, Mohr. Our task is to protect the rail line from terrorist attacks, which means constant patrolling. I'm still disabled by my wounds, so I'm afraid you will have your fill of walking in the woods. The company is also badly under strength at present; half the men were detached to a battle group for the Kursk offensive. I don't expect to see any of them again.'

He paused again, frowning. 'In fact, I doubt you've been made fully aware of the strategic situation, so I will summarise. July's Operation Citadel was a complete failure; it's the Russians who are on the front foot now and we who are doing the retreating. One thrust threatens Kharkov, while another heads west towards Orel. Thanks to our glorious Führer's masterly strategy, we have lost most of the forces that would have stopped the Russians, particularly…' Weimann suddenly stopped speaking. 'Ah, I see you are not immune to the charms of Frau Grabowski.'

Mohr, who had been wilting under Weimann's withering appraisal, had indeed had his attention diverted. A young woman had appeared briefly at the far end of the room as she passed through. Her clothing could not have been simpler: a faded blue peasant's smock hung from her slim shoulders while a pale checked headscarf covered her hair. Despite the brevity of her appearance, or even because of it, Mohr sensed around her an aura that owed nothing to working the land. Perhaps it was just the unexpected nature of her appearance, but he felt as though he had just seen a vision.

Seeing Mohr's surprise, Weimann explained. 'The dacha belongs to the Grabowskis. They live here as a temporary measure, which almost certainly means the duration of the war. They cultivate their own plot of land but they are certainly not peasants. I suspect they are from the Polish aristocratic class, but I don't press the matter.'

Belying his stern appearance, Weimann's voice was pleasantly modulated as he continued his disjointed briefing. 'More importantly, their produce provides some welcome variety to our rations. We'll have dinner here one evening and I'll introduce you to Grabowski. He's the only civilised man to be found this side of the Vistula; educated, cultured, a chess player and speaks excellent German.' Reflecting on his good fortune, he added, 'War is full of vicissitudes, Mohr, so we must take our small pleasures where we can. Grabowski may be a Pole, perhaps even a Jew, but he could be the chief rabbi for all I care. It would make no difference to me.'

Weimann paused briefly, choosing his words with extreme care. 'For some reason, Frau Grabowski never joins us at dinner, preferring to eat in the kitchen although she prepares all the meals. There's another curiosity, too: she never speaks. That is to say, not to me or the men on guard duty. At first I thought she might be mute, but I soon heard her talking to her husband. Nor will she look you in the eye, although that might just be excessive modesty. But I find it very strange.'

Weimann had lapsed into something of a reverie, from

which he suddenly emerged. 'That's enough for now. I'm billeted here but I'm afraid there's only room for one, so you'll be in the blockhouse. Sergeant Gross is the senior NCO; he will brief you on company orders and housekeeping. He's a good man but too old, really, for infantry work. And he has a family in Dusseldorf, so he worries about the bombing.'

Deeply despondent, Mohr left the dacha and headed for the blockhouse. The posting was proving even worse than he had anticipated. It seemed he had to suffer a superior officer half crippled by wounds and who showed little sign of the informality of his previous post, where even the colonel had called him Ernst. And what was a major, even a wounded one, doing in command of such a trifling unit, and so openly disparaging about the Führer?

Mohr had to duck to enter the lowered door of the blockhouse and banged his head in doing so.

~

At least Sergeant Gross lived up to Weimann's opinion. He had been at the blockhouse since the spring and exercised firm control of what remained of the company: disciplined, but not oppressively so. He was a kindly man, sometimes tinged with sadness, and he made it his task to ease Mohr into his duties as swiftly as possible. These were straightforward enough but the reduced company strength, Gross explained, was restricting their operational capabilities. Night patrols had been reduced, as had anti-terrorist sweeps. Until they received reinforcements it was all they could be expected to do. It did not help that the trains ran haphazardly, the vagaries of the war rendering any timetable meaningless. There was another problem too: wireless communication with headquarters was intermittent at best, the signals often lost in the sandy soil of the forest-clad hills.

This was far from reassuring, although it soon became clear to Mohr that the blockhouse had previously been regarded as a fairly soft posting. Terrorist activity had been only occasional and consequently patrolling was dull but relatively safe. As is the way with soldiers, the small garrison had made themselves as comfortable as possible. There had been a former forestry worker within their ranks who had proved an adept poacher, so venison and other game helped vary their rations. But the poacher had been sent with the others to the Kursk battle, and now intelligence reports showed terrorist activity increasing as the days shortened.

Mohr reported to the dacha every day, where Weimann introduced him to Grabowski. A slight, wiry figure, a little above average height, Grabowski was burdened with a lean, boyish face that belied his thirty-something years. Despite his agricultural labours, he was always clean shaven and presentable, as though striving to maintain a certain status. To Mohr he was pleasant but reserved, exhibiting a wariness that reflected his awkward situation.

Frau Grabowski remained a shy, reclusive figure, glimpsed rather than seen. When in the dacha, she preferred the sanctuary of her large kitchen, which both Weimann and Mohr respected as her inviolable private domain. To Mohr, her presence in the dacha seemed to possess a spectral quality, fleeting and insubstantial, as if the painting of the Virgin Mary that adorned the living room wall sometimes came to life.

Grabowski and his wife spent most of their time tending a cultivated strip that lay between the dacha and an extensive mixed orchard that reached as far as the hamlet. The part of the orchard closest to the hamlet seemed to be shared with the villagers. Indeed, as Weimann pointed out, there was a distinct seigneurial element in the relationship between Grabowski and the villagers, for they treated him with considerable deference and occasionally sought his advice. They also relied on him to act as a spokesman in their relations with the Germans.

Contact between the troops and the villagers was supposed to be minimal but in practice Gross, and now Mohr, turned a blind eye to the men's frequent forays for whatever fresh produce the villagers were willing to sell. Mohr also noticed another feature of the hamlet: there were no males present between the ages of fourteen and sixty-five, but he declined to ask why.

Mohr's duties were not onerous and his rapid absorption into the company was largely due to Gross, whose quietly imparted advice he found invaluable. It helped that he was not afraid to ask questions, being only too aware of his comparative inexperience. But in his discussions with Gross, Mohr soon detected an unspoken concern. Despite the elaborate conversion of the barn into a fortified blockhouse, it became clear that Gross regarded the dacha as a weak point. While it stood it had to be defended, and it would be better if it were not there.

Under the guise of a newcomer's curiosity, Mohr mentioned the matter to Major Weimann. His query received short shrift. There were sufficient men to defend the dacha and it lay hardly a hundred metres from the blockhouse, well within the scope of mutually supporting fire. Mohr pursued the subject no further but took the trouble to pace out the distance between the two buildings. Even allowing for the imprecision of his measurement, he calculated the distance at one hundred and forty metres, considerably more than Weimann's dismissive assertion. It would be a long way to run if the dacha had to be evacuated under fire, particularly for a cripple. But Major Weimann's word was law.

∞

It was barely a week after Mohr's arrival that Weimann gave him an order in the form of a request. This was most unusual; normally his orders, however few or trivial, were notably precise. But on this occasion Weimann was distinctly circumlocutory. 'I'm concerned about my wounds, Mohr. They are not healing as well as they should. Durst does his best, I know. He's not a bad medic but he's clumsy. There is still shrapnel in my leg and side, and it keeps working its way out, so there are constant new sores. Other pieces remain fixed but continually discharge. It makes for a very tedious business.'

'It sounds very unpleasant,' said Mohr, conscious that his own injuries had healed perfectly.

'It needs a more delicate touch than a heavy-handed soldier can provide, however well intentioned.'

'Yes,' agreed Mohr uncertainly, not clear where this was leading.

'Frau Grabowski would tend them very well, I think.'

'Yes,' said Mohr again, still uncertain. 'Do you know if she has any medical training? Been a nurse, perhaps?'

'I hardly think that matters. The work is not technical, it simply requires common sense and a delicate, sympathetic touch. Frau Grabowski would seem most suitable.'

'Yes, it would certainly appear so.'

'Then have a word with Grabowski, will you?' There was no doubt an order was contained within the request.

Mohr was embarrassed to continue. 'Do you think Herr Grabowski will agree? After all, we have our own medics and even hospital facilities, should they prove necessary.'

'Nonsense, Mohr. I've had enough of hospitals. I can't see any difficulty. Grabowski has always been willing to help us with any requests so far and I can't see why that should change now. Make it sound as though you are concerned for my welfare.'

Although vexed why Weimann – who spoke frequently

with Grabowski on cordial terms – could not make his own request, Mohr could see he had no choice in the matter. But the prospect was distasteful. His irritation that Weimann was using him was exacerbated by his reluctance to intrude into the Grabowskis' domestic affairs. His own relationship with Grabowski was superficial at best, usually just an acknowledgement and a mundane exchange about the weather. With Frau Grabowski, it was non-existent. He usually saw her in the distance, working among the lines of vegetables and fruit bushes, often wielding a hoe or gathering a basket of produce. Under the late summer sun, it always struck Mohr as a picture of rustic idealism that would have been appreciated by the French romantic painters. She made a compelling subject, for Mohr had seen her well enough to register her classical looks, with her rich chestnut hair tied back to display a delicate oval face and her skin as flawless as fine porcelain. And despite her plain, unflattering peasant garb, there was no disguising Frau Grabowski's feminine form beneath.

In the event, the request went better than Mohr could have expected. Reporting to the dacha one morning, he found Weimann absent, taking one of his laboured constitutional walks around the periphery of the property. Grabowski was present, although there was no sign of his wife, which suited Mohr. After a brief exchange of pleasantries, Mohr surprised himself at the ease with which he made the request. Just as Weimann had suggested, he couched it in terms of concern for his superior officer. Grabowski showed no surprise; indeed, he never exhibited much in the way of emotion, at least not to the Germans. Mohr managed to avoid any further involvement by suggesting Grabowski best speak directly to the major. An offer of Frau Grabowski's assistance would, he believed, be greatly appreciated.

Whatever Grabowski thought of the idea, he soon

spoke to Weimann and it was arranged. Frau Grabowski became Weimann's nurse. At first the daily ministrations were carried out in the kitchen but Weimann soon asserted that this was an unwarranted intrusion into her private sanctuary; besides, there was no comfortable chair on which he could recline while being treated. There was also a window through which he could see the guards. In his necessary state of undress, that was clearly unsatisfactory. It would be best if the treatment were conducted in his room. This statement – it was hardly a proposal for discussion – was directed at Grabowski rather than his wife. And so the arrangement changed, although the Grabowskis' view was known only to them.

ત

Weimann soon gave over – one might almost say abdicated – the responsibility for the company to Mohr but, while giving the routine operational matters only cursory attention, he retained a sharp interest in the company's discipline. In particular, he resolutely opposed any fraternisation with the local populace. The troops were forbidden to speak to the villagers, which placed Mohr in an awkward position because this order was more honoured in the breach since the men continued to barter for food.

The village was strictly out of bounds to off-duty soldiers, so when Mohr had to report that two men had been caught there after dark, Weimann was predictably incensed. 'Who was it?' he demanded.

'Fritsche and Hofmeister, sir.'

'That pair again! They are the worst defaulters in the company. Hofmeister is easily led, simple-minded in my view. But Fritsche is a menace. It's only because he had a sprained ankle that he wasn't included in the battlegroup draft, more's the pity.'

Weimann's annoyance had made him red in the face,

something Mohr had not observed before. 'You'll have to deal with it, Mohr. If I see Fritsche again I'll lose my temper and he'll be straight on his way to a disciplinary battalion. The trouble is, we can't afford to lose any more men, even the likes of Fritsche.'

As if to recompense Mohr for burdening him with the unanticipated role of company commander, or perhaps in return for Mohr's help regarding Frau Grabowski, Weimann suddenly extended an invitation. 'On to more pleasant business. Now that you're settled in, we must have dinner together one evening. Grabowski should be able to join us. Some civilised conversation, a welcome break from the vicissitudes of war.' It was an expression Mohr had heard him use before.

❧

When Mohr reported to the dacha for dinner, he took the precaution of taking a gift. It was a bottle of Napoleon brandy, a luxury brought all the way from his posting in France. Despite Mohr's misgivings, the gift was well received by Weimann. 'Ah, I see you are a man of some discernment, Mohr. This is far better than the dreadful vin ordinaire I've been able to obtain. A cognac bearing the name of a military genius – what could be more appropriate? Perhaps some of the genius will rub off on us, for we certainly need it.' Weimann led the way to the table. 'I regret I have been unable to persuade Grabowski to join us, nor his wife, of course. She is preparing the food, however, so we shall be quite spoilt.'

Mohr's heart sank at the prospect of an entire evening solely in Weimann's company. Grabowski's presence would, he felt, have offered considerably more scope to the conversation. In fact, their talk began on the most mundane of subjects, a report on the company's military activities that day. But Weimann – for it quickly became clear he would do most of the talking – soon digressed into broader subjects, although still of a military nature. He expounded on the dilution of the German army's strength by the inclusion of less-competent allies such as the Italians, Hungarians and Romanians. Was Mohr aware that even Ukrainians were being recruited now?

Mohr was vaguely aware but expressed surprise at such a development. They must hate the Russians greatly to volunteer for an occupier's army, he surmised. Weimann's reply was blunt: it was a choice of military service, forced labour or starvation. Faced with these choices, volunteering for the German army was understandable, but it made for poor soldiers. Mohr listened dutifully, occasionally adding his own uncontroversial remarks.

In the unexplained absence of Grabowski, his wife not only prepared the meal but delivered it to the table. Whenever she appeared the two men fell silent, apparently inhibited by her presence although for no discernible reason. As usual she did not speak, concerning herself solely with delivering each dish as unobtrusively and swiftly as possible. But Frau Grabowski's presence was inescapable. Mohr was acutely conscious of her close proximity as she waited table with silent, self-effacing efficiency. He avoided looking at her, merely muttering his thanks as courses came and went. Weimann was also quiet, a reticence that struck Mohr as very odd in a man usually so self-assured.

At the conclusion of the meal, Weimann thanked Frau Grabowski. As she cleared the last dishes from the table, he addressed her directly. 'Thank you, Frau Grabowski, a most splendid meal much appreciated by us both.'

She stood stock still while he spoke, plates poised in her hands as though in suspended animation. Although her understanding of German was doubtful, Mohr thought he detected the tiniest movement of her head in acknowledgement before she disappeared back into the kitchen. No doubt Weimann's tone had given sufficient indication of his meaning.

Mohr could not help wondering what lay behind the Grabowskis' bland mask. He found it extraordinarily difficult to imagine what level of subservience should be shown to an invader, even a civilised one. He wondered what attitude he would adopt in their situation and found no easy answer.

By the time the first glasses of cognac were dispensed after their meal, Mohr was becoming well acquainted with Weimann's service. In spite of himself, he found much of Weimann's story interesting, if only because it shed light on events that had occurred in Mohr's adolescence and about which he was largely ignorant. Weimann had persevered with the army through the dog years of the Versailles Treaty restrictions imposed after the Great War. Hitler's accession to power had marked the turning point, and then the Spanish civil war had provided opportunities for an ambitious officer. There he had been blooded in the dark arts of war.

That experience was further honed in Poland and France, so that when Russia was invaded he was confident of total victory. 'We should have defeated the Russians in 1941, or '42 at the latest. Now it is difficult to be optimistic.' Weimann lapsed into reminiscence. 'You should have been there, Mohr, in the early days. The unstoppable panzer breakthroughs, the huge encirclements, whole Russian armies cut off, surrounded and then surrendered. Day after day pushing east, often catching Soviet units still assembling, completely unaware we were so close. Those were great days. If our great Führer had played it correctly, the Russians would have been finished.'

He took a generous swig of his brandy then studied the glass glinting in the low light of the oil lamp. 'Yes, those were the days. They would gladden the heart of any professional soldier, regardless of nationality. Crossing endless tracts of land that stretched east like a vast inland sea. Huge rivers were just obstacles to be overcome: the Dnieper, the Don and, finally, the Volga. My regiment was among the first to reach the Volga, on the high ground north of Stalingrad. We think the Rhine is a mighty river, Mohr, even the biggest in the world. But the Volga – now there is a river. Two, even three kilometres wide, studded with islands, some of them large and inhabited. An untamed river, completely different from our engineered waterways, which are mere streams in comparison.'

Weimann gazed into his glass, content in his reminiscences. 'I admit there were times when we were fearful, afraid some counter-attacking masterstroke could send us hurtling back. But the counter-attacks were defeated, the advance resumed and it was impossible not to feel uplifted by the whole experience. We saw the Bolsheviks crumbling before us and felt … well, we felt like Siegfried.'

Mohr heard this soliloquy with fascination; it threw into sharp relief the difference between a professional soldier and a conscript. His planned career in architecture, he realised, had nothing to compare with this Wagnerian epic. And still Weimann had not finished.

'As we looked across the Volga, the whole of Russia and Siberia seemed to lie before us, even to the Pacific coast. But when you look at an atlas, Mohr, you see how much further there was to travel. We weren't even a quarter of the way. That's when the doubts began to form, unspoken of course, but there nonetheless. I was wounded at Stalingrad and flown out just as we were encircled. I was one of the lucky ones.' He paused for a moment, contemplating the fate of an entire German army. But Mohr found his next revelation even more surprising.

'I expect you wonder why a senior major should be

commanding such a trifling unit here in the middle of nowhere. Particularly when you realise that my contemporaries – those who have survived – are now colonels and even generals. Why am I languishing here, Mohr?' He leaned forward, as if divulging a conspiracy. 'It's because I have some damn-fool relatives, that's why. An uncle and his son – the one a retired colonel and the other a serving officer – have been stupid enough to voice their disapproval of the Nazis. Not once, you understand, but a number of times. They have associated with others of like mind and, like all these groups, have come to the attention of the Gestapo. And because we bear the same name, we have all become suspects, tainted by our common blood.'

Weimann leaned back in his chair, as though confession had purged his mind. 'Fortunately, the colonel of this regiment is a friend of my family. When he heard of fresh Gestapo enquiries he acted at once, extricating me from convalescence in Kiev and bringing me here, where I am apparently orchestrating crucial operations against the terrorists. His theory is that this far east, and doing such vital work, the Gestapo will stay their hand. But I know I'm finished as a regular soldier working for promotion. Here I fill my time writing notes on the campaigns in which I've taken part, evaluating what we got right and wrong, hoping it might be useful for some officers' course in the future. This is my military lot now: beating the forest for bandits who disdain to wear uniform and try to shoot you in the back. It is not war as I was trained to fight it.'

He fell silent, consoled solely by the presence of Napoleon in the brandy he rolled gently around his glass. Mohr was also silent, having nothing to say to rival his superior's monologue.

In the end it was Weimann, perhaps wearying of self-pity, who changed the subject. 'Do you have a girlfriend,

Mohr, or perhaps even a fiancée?'

'No,' replied Mohr, surprised at the sudden change of conversation. 'No, I don't.' In view of Weimann's strictures on fraternisation, he felt it best not to admit that his most recent girlfriend had been French, and that they still corresponded.

Weimann continued, 'I have a wife and daughter, living near Munich. My wife has family there. It's too far south for the Allied bombers to reach, so they're relatively safe for the time being. You're lucky to be single at such a time. Family is bad for a soldier, a powerful distraction from the job in hand.'

'How old is your daughter?' asked Mohr, keen to divert the talk from military matters.

'She's six, and very much like her mother: beautiful when quiet.'

'Do you have a photograph?'

'No, I don't.' Weimann contemplated his glass of cognac, as if wondering whether to explain this apparent deficiency. Without looking at Mohr he continued, 'You must think that strange but there is a good reason. You see, I doubt whether I am the girl's father.'

Mohr felt as though he had been doused with ice-cold water. This was too much, but Weimann wasn't finished. 'My wife tried to convince me that the dates were possible but it's very unlikely. It would require a nine-and-a-half-month pregnancy, and relations on the last day or so before I returned to Spain, which I certainly don't recall. It might just be possible, perhaps, but extremely unlikely. And it ignores another fact, that she finds the attentions of other men not unwelcome. Put yourself in my place, Mohr. What would you think?'

Mohr was too embarrassed to speak so Weimann, perhaps encouraged by the brandy, added, 'I can't say I blame the woman. Being a soldier's wife is a special calling and she just doesn't have it. The long absences, the loneliness – I understand the difficulties but I can't stand the deceit. It would have been better if she'd admitted the truth; I could have lived with that. The girl is delightful, so I would have been prepared to bring her up as my own. But my wife's deviousness is an insurmountable obstacle.'

His face broke into a thin, humourless smile. 'You should think yourself lucky, Mohr, that you don't carry such burdens. But female companionship is necessary at times, don't you think?'

This time Mohr managed a minimal reply. 'Yes, it certainly has its attractions.'

'Exactly so,' murmured Weimann, his voice more confidential. 'But the attractiveness of women can take many forms. Take Frau Grabowski, for example. Did you ever see such an angelic creature? Despite constant manual labour and the dullest of clothes, she has an extraordinary beauty, don't you think? It really is quite remarkable. And she has the most gentle touch when dressing my wounds, which are responding already. And yet she never speaks, even when we are alone in my room. Grabowski says she doesn't understand German but I'm not entirely convinced. It would be rare for an intelligent Pole not to understand a word of German. Perhaps I can overcome her reticence with a blitzkrieg of German charm.'

Mohr was desperate to escape. 'It's time I checked the sentries, Herr Major.'

As he stepped down from the dacha's veranda Mohr paused, exhaling a deep sigh of relief. Strolling to the bunker at the corner of the dacha, he exchanged a few words with the guards before bidding them goodnight. Then, as he carefully edged his way past the wood store, he suddenly sensed a denser blackness against the shadowed timber wall. For a moment he thought it was another sentry, before realising that the slim figure must be Frau

Grabowski. He stopped, aware that she was looking at him although her face was hidden by the darkness. After an indeterminate silence he felt obliged to speak but, before he could do so, the figure turned and disappeared into the dacha through the kitchen door.

Mohr stared after her, feeling that Frau Grabowski had acknowledged him for the first time.

❧

The patrol picked its way slowly along the railway line, four men checking the track and two sections either side in the forest. Mohr was among the trees, indistinguishable from the men because he had hidden his badges of rank on the advice of Sergeant Gross. 'We know who you are but a sniper won't.'

Despite his initial reservations, Mohr had come to terms with patrolling. It allowed him to escape the claustrophobic blockhouse. Out in the forest there was a greater sense of comradeship, a recognition of their interdependence. He had also come to appreciate the beauty of the landscape, for the birches and willows were already turning multiple shades of yellow and gold in the soft September light. Soon the first frost would come, harbinger of many more to follow.

Picking his way carefully through the trees, Mohr came across a defensible hollow and signalled a meal break. Corporal Pelz posted the sentries while the rest of the men set about their rations. On Pelz's return, Mohr offered to share a hard-boiled egg, a gift from the blockhouse cook. Pelz grinned and shook his head, producing one of his own. Mohr reflected that he should have known better. Despite his squint and unmilitary appearance, Pelz was natural soldier on whom Mohr relied almost as much as he did on Gross.

Having finished his rations, Mohr stood up and

walked a short distance into the trees. He still found it uncomfortable to perform natural functions in view of the men. When he had finished, he drew back towards the hollow but then stopped, standing alone beside a dense holly bush for a moment. He could hear low voices coming from the hollow, faint but distinguishable to a keen ear. Realising he might hear something uncomplimentary about himself, he thought it might be best to return but a voice made him pause.

'Have you finished your extra guards yet, Fritsche?'

'Two more to do.'

'And was it worth it?'

'I should say so. My Polska mama might not be much to look at but she's a real goer, as sex-starved as they come. Hardly surprising, as there's no men about.'

'How come she saw you then,' said another voice, 'if she was looking for a man?'

'I've got it where it counts, that's why.'

Fresh voices were coming thick and fast. 'We've all seen what you've got, Fritsche. My dachshund's better hung.'

'Balls. When it's up, mine is bigger than your dachshund. And it's what you do with it that counts. That's what my Polska mama appreciates.'

'She won't be able to appreciate it when you get sent to a punishment battalion.'

'Rubbish. What harm is there in being friendly with the natives?'

'You'll be pushing your luck if you're caught again.'

'I'm not saying I'll do it again – at least, not in front of Corporal Pelz. I'm just saying I don't see the harm, that's all.' Fritsche's tone changed as he added, 'Besides, if it's no fraternisation for us, it should apply to everyone.'

'What are you on about?'

'You know what I mean. One rule for the men and another for the officers.'

'No, we don't know. Tell us.'

'Use your eyes, man. It's obvious. Next time you do a guard at the dacha, use your eyes.'

'She's treating his wounds instead of Durst,' claimed another voice. 'Anyone can see he's still a cripple.'

'Yes, of course. But for an hour at a time, upstairs, hidden away in his room?'

'Shut it, Fritsche!' Pelz's voice cut through the air like a knife. 'Shut it, or I'll make sure your next stop is a punishment battalion, never mind the major.'

Standing by the holly bush, Mohr was appalled. The worst of it was, he could see Fritsche's point, however crassly put. But if that was the feeling among the rest of the men… Squirming at the thought, he hurried back to the hollow where silence was giving way to muted conversations.

'You really should take a buddy with you,' said Pelz very quietly. 'It's standard procedure. I know there are sentries but it's orders and, if you don't, it sends the wrong message to the men. You'll soon get used to it.' He grinned to soften the criticism. 'One other thing, sir, if I may. We've been here for nearly twenty-five minutes. It's too long. Fifteen minutes, twenty at most, and then we should be on the move again. That way there's less opportunity for them to set up an ambush.'

Mohr nodded in acknowledgement but without enthusiasm.

'Don't take it hard, sir, we all have to learn. Sergeant Gross, myself, we've had to learn the hard way. Many of our comrades have paid the learning price.' Pelz fell silent for a moment before giving Mohr a friendly smile. 'You're doing fine, sir. It's good that we've got an active officer among us.'

'Thank you, corporal. You'd better move us out.'

Pelz looked round before speaking up. 'Where's our love

warrior? Yes, you Fritsche. Get yourself on point and lead us off. Imagine the terrorists as lonely hausfraus and you'll sniff them out in no time.'

※

Mohr did not always accompany the rail-track patrols. There were minor administrative duties to perform, the inescapable paperwork that bedevils so many organisations, including armies. But this role was not onerous for a tidy mind, nor overly time consuming, and so he was left with a good deal of spare time. To escape the stale, rank atmosphere of the blockhouse, it became his habit to seek seclusion in the nearby orchard. There, sitting with his back against a favoured pear tree, he found brief interludes of peaceful solitude where he could read and reply to letters from home and friends.

If there was no correspondence to attend to, Mohr simply let his mind wander where it would, sometimes even fall asleep in the last of the year's warmth. He also read, an eclectic mix ranging from his own two books on architecture – in which he was disturbed to find he had lost interest – to a variety of books borrowed from the men. There was a recognised system of passing books around, everything from trashy novels to occasional reference books or an anthology of poetry. Mohr appreciated them all for they provided welcome, if temporary, relief from the war.

But there was no real escape from the war. Even in his orchard sanctuary he could hear the trains passing by. Those heading east carried men and armaments to the front: long, slow trains drawing primitive carriages crammed with blank-faced troops interspersed with low flatcars bearing the shrouded outlines of tanks and guns. At least those trains offered the blockhouse troops some reassurance that the Russian offensives could be stopped and relief that, for the moment, they were spared that same journey to the front.

It was the westbound trains that they loathed. All too frequent, and depressingly long, these bore the wounded. Every man averted his eyes as they passed but, if the wind was in the wrong direction, nothing could expunge the brief, pervasive smell of blood, pus and disinfectant. Even hidden in his orchard hideaway, Mohr was not spared this visceral reminder of what fate might ultimately await the blockhouse garrison.

Nevertheless, these sojourns in the orchard were still much favoured by Mohr. And it was there one mild, cloudy day that his attention was drawn to a flock of small birds busily working their way among the orchard tree tops, travellers to the south since the frosts had started to make their presence felt. As he listening to the cheerful chirruping and watched their short, restless flights among the branches, he suddenly became aware of another visitor. This one was perfectly still, standing beside a pear tree, half hidden in the shadows under the thinning leaf canopy. Silent and unmoving, Frau Grabowski seemed even more like an apparition as she watched him. He had no idea how long she had been there. Nor was he sure whether she realised he had seen her.

For a moment each observed the other. Mohr wondered whether she wanted to speak, or if he should speak to her. But the wraith-like figure suddenly turned away and disappeared among the trees, leaving Mohr baffled and somehow frustrated, as though an opportunity had been lost. Was it just chance that had brought her here? It occurred to him that, since he visited this same place with some regularity, she might have watched him and he hadn't noticed, such was his inattention while reading or daydreaming. The thought unsettled him, as though his privacy had been invaded. He was left with the inescapable impression that Frau Grabowski wanted to communicate with him, and he found that thought equally unsettling.

※

Mohr felt impelled to visit the dacha a little more frequently in subsequent days, looking particularly for Frau Grabowski. He was careful not to make it obvious, stating to Weimann that, with growing risk of attack, he was concerned to see that the guards' vigilance reflected the increasing threat. He also suggested minor improvements to the dacha's sandbag defences, to which Weimann responded with scarcely veiled indifference since he had overseen the original measures.

It was during these visits that Mohr came to realise Weimann's attention to his military role was gradually slipping. Questions about the rail-track patrols, the state of the blockhouse and even the men, which had been the source of regular penetrating enquiries only a few weeks earlier, were now much less frequent and more perfunctory. Perhaps the major was satisfied with Mohr's capabilities, although Mohr's relative inexperience made this unlikely to a soldier of Weimann's service. And Weimann had taken to having his wounds dressed sometimes twice a day, despite claiming they were improving 'beyond measure'. In the privacy of his room, Major Weimann often spent more than an hour a day attended by Frau Grabowski, whose silent ministrations were apparently proving so beneficial.

Mohr's attempts to see Frau Grabowski at the dacha were unsuccessful. Yes, there were the usual occasional glimpses but no opportunity to catch her eye, let alone speak. And his visits to the orchard were now curtailed by a change to the weather. October is the time of the autumn rasputitsa, when rain and early snow turn the unmade roads into quagmires. In military terms, it is also known as 'General Mud', a formidable, if neutral, adversary.

But the sun still sometimes broke through and, one day when it did, Mohr hastened to his place in the orchard. He made his going obvious, first visiting the dacha guards before strolling over there. The Grabowskis, working in the distance, took no notice of him. Nonetheless, when Mohr settled against his pear tree he could not concentrate. Having no letters to read or write, he had brought a book but it lay open in his lap, unread. At frequent intervals he looked out from under his eyebrows until, after an hour, he despaired of her coming.

It was only as he prepared to leave that he realised she was there. He had put his book in his jacket pocket, stood up and picked up the folded groundsheet on which he had been sitting. It was only as he turned to leave that he saw her. She was closer this time, although still clinging to the illusory security of the shadows. This time Mohr took the initiative. 'Frau Grabowski, can I help? Do you wish to speak to me?'

Receiving no reply, Mohr again took the initiative and closed the gap between them. 'Do you understand German?'

'Vous devez m'aider.' Her voice was quiet but insistent.

For a moment Mohr did not understand but French was familiar from his recent service there, and his grasp of the language slowly reasserted itself.

'You must help me.' She said it again, willing him to understand.

'Yes, but how?' He replied in French, fervently hoping it was comprehensible, for there was an air of supplication in her manner.

'He uses me.' She spoke slowly, to ensure understanding.

Mohr stared at the figure in front of him, subconsciously registering the beautiful but earnest face. Had he understood correctly? 'Who uses you, Madame?'

'He uses me,' she repeated, unwilling or unable to utter a name. Then she spoke more quickly and Mohr had to unscramble the words. One struck him like a bullet: enceinte.

The import of her words rendered him speechless. If he had understood correctly – and her words were few and concise – his superior officer had forced himself on this woman and now she believed she was pregnant. He raised a hand to his mouth, aghast at the implications.

'Vous devez m'aider,' she said again, the meaning unmistakable. And then she turned on her heels and was gone, almost running between the uncaring trees.

He gathered up his things and started walking back to the blockhouse. Had he understood Frau Grabowski correctly? After all, it was months since he had spoken French regularly and he had never been fluent. But in his soul Mohr knew he understood only too clearly. The only mystery was how she could attribute the pregnancy to Major Weimann with such certainty. That was very odd. He supposed there were plausible explanations. Perhaps the Grabowskis had agreed to postpone having children until more favourable times, or Grabowski was infertile, or even impotent. But whatever the explanation, Mohr believed her; a glimpse of her barely controlled anguish brooked not the slightest doubt.

But her plea for help – what on earth was he supposed to do? What could he do? The idea of speaking to Weimann about the subject filled him with a dread almost worse than the terrorists. And what could he say; what solutions offered themselves? That she be sent away to relatives, if they existed? An abortion by an army doctor? The ideas flitted through his brain, consistent only in their utter implausibility.

As he reached the blockhouse, Mohr sensed a change of atmosphere. The few men outside seemed subdued and did not speak, which was unusual. He ducked under the doorway into the gloomy interior. Sergeant Gross stood beside the signaller, their expressions as sombre as the men outside.

'We have received a message from regimental HQ,' said Gross quietly. 'We have to provide men for a battle group. They have intelligence about the location of a terrorist camp in the forest and an immediate operation has been ordered. You have to report to Major Weimann for orders.'

'Aren't you included?' asked Mohr, puzzled at the omission.

'No.' Gross shook his head. 'You have to report to Major Weimann immediately. The transport is coming this afternoon.'

Mohr set off for the dacha where he found Weimann quite animated, the news of the forthcoming raid having apparently restored his focus. He came straight to the point. 'Gross has told you, I imagine?'

'Yes, Herr Major.'

'We have to detach at least twenty men to this battle group. They wanted more but I argued we are already at less than half establishment. It will leave us with just twenty-six men, sufficient to cover for the two or three days anticipated for the operation. It will mean us suspending most of our patrolling along the rail track and restricting activity to no more than a kilometre radius from the blockhouse.' Weimann paused. 'You should be taking notes, Mohr, unless you have supreme confidence in your memory.'

When Mohr had finished fumbling in his jacket for a notebook and pencil, Weimann continued. 'Keep Gross and Pelz here, and don't send all our best men. And, despite what I've said about him in the past, keep Fritsche; he's a nuisance but a good soldier.'

Mohr scribbled away, although Weimann soon went

beyond orders into giving advice. This Mohr found this increasingly irritating. Assisted by Gross and Pelz, he had been running the company perfectly well for weeks, with Weimann noticeable principally by his absence. Now, from the obscurity of the dacha, the man was dispensing the sort of advice that even a recently converted infantry leutnant could be expected to know.

His irritation had a consequence. When Weimann declared the briefing over, Mohr put away his notebook and pencil but made no move to leave. Instead, with a determination founded on both annoyance and deep disquiet, he addressed Weimann's back. 'Herr Major, may I speak with you on another matter?'

Weimann looked round. 'What is it?'

'I believe Frau Grabowski is concerned about continuing to treat your wounds.'

'What are you talking about, Mohr?' Weimann's face clouded in disbelief. 'How would you know?'

'I happened to see her. We bumped into each other in the orchard. We couldn't communicate very well, but she implied her continuing treatment is causing difficulties with her husband.'

Weimann's face contorted in anger. 'I'm astonished, Mohr. First, that you speak Polish, something you seem to have concealed until now, and, second, that you have the effrontery to discuss my personal arrangements with Frau Grabowski.'

Mohr had no option but to press on. 'She speaks French, Herr Major, and she must have heard that I served in France and assumed I spoke it too. She doesn't speak German. I can only think that's why she spoke to me.'

'And how long have these cosy chats in the orchard been going on?'

'Only once, Herr Major, just today.'

'You expect me to believe that?' Weimann glared at his

junior officer, his face flushed.

'It happens to be true, Herr Major,' replied Mohr, unable to offer any other answer.

Weimann was about to speak but suddenly changed his mind. There was a long silence during which he switched his gaze from Mohr to somewhere in the middle distance. His face betrayed small involuntary movements, as though afflicted by some barely controlled emotion. But when he finally spoke, his voice was strangely quiet. 'Get back to your duties; this is no time for such matters.'

Mohr saluted and turned to leave the dacha. As he reached the door, he heard Weimann's voice from behind him. 'You have been disloyal, Mohr, an unforgiveable trait in a German officer.'

And you have been despicable, thought Mohr, but he declined to say so.

∞

Back in the blockhouse, he conferred with Sergeant Gross. They drew up a list of personnel and equipment for the battle group and ordered two lance corporals to pass the word around. Since Corporal Pelz was already out with a patrol, the selection fell on those remaining at the blockhouse so there was little opportunity to pick and choose as Weimann had ordered.

As they worked together, Mohr sensed Gross's concern and tried to anticipate its cause. 'Do you think we are left with enough men?'

Gross considered carefully before answering. 'Yes, I think so, but it's the bare minimum.' Reviving his old concern, he went on. 'We have to cover the dacha as well as the blockhouse, which makes it a stretch. As the major says, provided we restrict daytime activity to the local area and increase the guard at night, we should get by. But I don't think there will be much sleep for anyone until the others return.'

'At least it's an opportunity to strike at the terrorists for a change. God knows, we've managed little enough of that.'

'Yes.' Gross sounded doubtful. 'Operations like this in the forest are difficult. We often end up chasing shadows, even though I assume there is a guide of some sort, an informer or a deserter. But let's hope they are successful. We need the partisans to suffer some setbacks if we are to keep the trains running.'

※

The transport arrived in the early afternoon, a single truck this time, led by the usual motorcycle combination. There was an air of suppressed tension among the troops, more so among the battle-group party. It was detectable in the muted banter, the sound of friendships being parted with contrived bravado but undermined by the uncertainty of their resumption.

As the lorry pulled away shouted exchanges quickly died to silence, although a few men continued to watch and wave until the lorry disappeared beyond the hamlet. Then they turned back to their duties, secretly glad the parting was over. The daylight was slipping away and the air became sharp with frost.

※

Mohr came awake to the crash of explosions and the sharp crack of incoming fire. Urgent voices echoed around the log walls of the blockhouse, accompanied by the heavy footfalls of men hurrying to their posts. Weapons were made ready with the dull-sharp clash of metal on metal. A voice shouted, 'Kill the lights! Quick, put out the lights!' Grabbing his helmet, Mohr was already out of his bunk when the blanket curtain was roughly pulled aside and a voice muttered, 'We're under attack, Herr Leutnant.'

'Yes,' responded Mohr, testy in his nervousness. 'I do know gunfire when I hear it.' But the man must have gone because there was no reply.

Mohr struggled to pull on his boots. Picking up his weapon, he started groping his way through the darkness to the command post. Somewhere outside, the crump of a mortar explosion shook dirt and dust from the blockhouse roof and he wondered whether it would withstand a direct hit. At one of the apertures a machine gunner fired a long burst into the darkness. Can he see a target, wondered Mohr. Or is he just seeking reassurance? From somewhere in the darkness Corporal Pelz' voice, unexpectedly harsh, cut through the darkness. 'Short bursts, gunner, or you'll burn out the barrel.' After a moment's pause, he added, 'Is that you, sir?'

'Yes, what's the situation?'

'They're firing from beyond the rail line, I think. And there's firing at the dacha, but I'm not sure what's happening there.'

'Where's Sergeant Gross?' Mohr suddenly realised who was missing. 'He's supposed to be on duty here.'

'He's outside, checking the trenches.'

At that moment a black figure ducked in through the sunken doorway. 'Herr Leutnant?'

'I'm here.'

'They're firing from the eastern tree line and beyond the rail track.' Gross sounded slightly out of breath. 'One mortar, perhaps three light machine guns and some rifles – hardly an invasion force, so far as I can tell. I can't be sure about the dacha, but there was some firing very close to it. We must check with them.'

Before Mohr could make his way to the field telephone, its harsh buzzer sounded through the blockhouse. He fumbled for the handset.

'Is that you, Mohr?' The tension was evident in Weimann's

voice.

'Yes, sir.'

'Listen, we're in some trouble here. They're right up against the house, by the wood-store. There are just four of us here now. Somehow they managed to approach the bunker and knock it out. Grabowski went out to check his livestock and the sentry must have thought it was him returning.' Weimann paused, then added, 'No matter; you must organise a counter-attack. Take half your men, double into the village and then come through the orchard and take them in the flank. Set up fire support from the blockhouse and we'll support you from this end. Let me know when you're ready.'

'Yes, sir.' Mohr wondered whether he needed any further details about the counter-attack. He found himself asking, 'Is Frau Grabowski there?'

'Of course. She's in the shelter. Now get organised and let me know when you're ready.'

Mohr heard the sound of the handset being replaced.

Someone had lit a single candle, screened on three sides by hessian sheets. The signaller was trying to call up regimental headquarters but with no response. Perhaps the aerial had been shot down.

Mohr turned to Gross. 'We've got to organise a counter-attack through the village and orchard. Half the men, Major Weimann says, with fire support from here and the dacha. The terrorists are right up against the house, and there are only four of ours left to defend it.'

In the faint, flickering light, Gross was unmoving, as if struck dumb.

'We have to hurry,' urged Mohr.

'They should break out of the dacha. It makes no sense for us to counter-attack. We have no idea what's out there.'

'But the major has given an order. We must do as he says. Besides, he couldn't possibly run with the others in a breakout. He wouldn't stand a chance.'

'Yes,' muttered Gross, but he did not move.

Frustrated, Mohr tried cajoling the sergeant into action. 'We have to go now. They need our help urgently.'

There was a noticeable delay before Gross replied flatly, 'If you take half the men out there, we will all be dead within an hour.'

'What do you mean?'

'Have you considered why they are firing from the tree line when the village is closer and just as easy to approach? Or why they haven't stormed the dacha already or, much simpler, set fire to it? It makes no sense, unless they are trying to draw us out of the blockhouse.'

Taken aback, Mohr could only repeat, 'But they need our help. The major has given an order.'

'I know, but this decision affects every man here, not just in the dacha.'

The implication of Gross's statement began to register with Mohr. 'But we can't be sure they're waiting for us. And what could I say to the major?'

After a moment's silence, Gross spoke with diplomatic precision. 'Major Weimann is a very experienced soldier. He chose this barn for the blockhouse and organised its conversion and defences. It was his decision to include the dacha in the defence perimeter. Now that we are under attack, he will understand the situation.'

'But I can't just say we're abandoning them, that we intend to do nothing.' There was more than a hint of desperation in Mohr's voice.

'It's difficult, Herr Leutnant, I understand that. But, in effect, you are in command now. You must decide for us all.'

Mohr rocked back on his heels, absorbing this unwanted responsibility. He turned to the signaller. 'Is there still nothing from HQ? Or another blockhouse?' On seeing a negative shake of the head, he added bitterly, 'Why don't they reply? Or are we expected to fight this war entirely on our own?'

'They can't relieve us, even if we get through,' muttered Gross, half to himself. 'The battle group is stuck in the forest and the terrorists know it. The camp information is almost certainly false, a clever set-up.'

Mohr stared at the sergeant, not wanting to believe him. The field telephone buzzed again. With deep reluctance Mohr picked up the handset.

'What's happening, Mohr?' the major demanded. 'Aren't you ready yet? What on earth is keeping you?'

'We're just making final preparations.'

'For God's sake get a move on. Remember, go wide through the village and then sweep through the orchard. They won't stand – they're just bandits, not regular troops.'

'Yes, Herr Major.' The line went dead and Mohr shrugged his shoulders at Gross. 'We'll have to do as he says. We have no choice.'

'Wait a minute.' Gross ducked through the door and disappeared outside. Mohr was suddenly aware the firing had died away to desultory single shots and occasional short bursts. The partisans' mortar had ceased fire. But no sooner had this registered with him than firing recommenced, among which Mohr was concerned to hear the dull crump of grenades indicating that the terrorists had managed to approach much closer.

Gross reappeared through the low door. 'The terrorists are working their way in for an attack on the blockhouse. They are approaching through dead ground beside the rail track and the village. A counter-attack is out of the question at the moment. That is what you must tell Major Weimann.'

Mohr stared hard at the sergeant. Was it a coincidence that the firing had renewed while Gross was outside? The firing became less intense; it was still persistent but it was difficult to pick out much incoming. He picked up the handset and gave a savage burst on the telephone's buzzer handle.

'What's happening, Mohr?'

He repeated what Gross had said and there was a long silence from the dacha end. When Weimann eventually spoke, his voice was surprisingly calm. 'Ah, I suspect the cautious sergeant Gross has made his influence felt. I can't say I'm surprised. It's a sad fact, Mohr, but the Wehrmacht is not the army of two years ago. Those men are dead, and we shall soon join them.'

Mohr had not the slightest idea what to say. The firing was slowly dying down again, which he found intensely embarrassing.

Weimann was not quite ready to end their conversation. 'Would you care to say goodbye to Frau Grabowski?'

It was like a physical blow to Mohr. 'Surely they won't kill her. She's Polish, for God's sake! Grabowski's wife.'

Weimann's harsh laugh echoed down the line. 'You've a lot to learn, Mohr.' Abruptly, he added, 'Tell me if the situation changes.' And then he was gone.

'Yes, sir,' whispered Mohr into the dead handset.

During the next three-quarters of an hour, the blockhouse defenders kept up intermittent fire with occasional more intense outbursts. Gross assumed command as Mohr sat, sunk in apathy. Eventually he roused himself sufficiently to ask when the terrorists might renew their attack.

Gross thought for a moment. 'They won't want to leave it late; they need to be well into the forest by daylight. As soon as they're certain we're not coming out of the blockhouse, there will be no point in putting it off.'

Gross was right. Half an hour before midnight, the terrorists renewed their attack. The blockhouse came under heavy fire, including three more rounds from the mortar.

But it was the dacha that suffered. Above the noise of their own fire, the blockhouse defenders could hear the furious assault, the crump of muffled explosions interspersed with sustained bursts of automatic fire. Mohr recovered himself and took up a position facing the dacha, blazing away blindly towards its flank in a hopeless gesture of support.

Nothing could prevent the sound of occasional human screams carrying to the blockhouse, primal, animal noises that made machine-gun fire sound almost wholesome. Mohr fired as much to try and block out the sounds as help his comrades, running through magazine after magazine until he had a stoppage. He suddenly realised that the dacha had fallen silent and the blockhouse slowly followed suit. Nobody spoke but, somewhere in the darkness, a man was quietly crying.

~

In the half light of dawn, Mohr over-ruled Gross and insisted on leading the patrol. Split into two sections, the second led by the squint-eyed Corporal Pelz, he instructed that only one section move at a time. Crawling from the blockhouse, the men of the patrol lay scattered and prone in the frosty dirt, tensed for the order to move. When it came, short, sprinted bounds carried them to the edge of the village where they paused to recover their breath and start probing around the hovels. Not a single villager stirred outside. They edged cautiously into the orchard, searching the ground for booby traps, but found only a few live rounds spilt in the darkness. There were also indentations in the grass beside the trees where the terrorists had waited in ambush.

Only Mohr and Pelz entered the dacha. The defenders had died at their inadequate, makeshift posts and lay crumpled and distorted like broken dolls. Weimann lay within arm's reach of the funk-hole under the stairs where

Frau Grabowski had sheltered. It was as if his final act had been in her defence. His body had been mutilated with bayonets and then carelessly fitted with a grenade booby-trap.

They found Frau Grabowski seated in the kitchen. She had been tied to a chair with meticulous thoroughness, from which there was never a hope of escape. A grenade had been secured in her lap which, with a five-seconds delay, gave the partisans sufficient time to exit the room. Explosions can be curiously serendipitous in their distribution of force; this one had left Frau Grabowski's face completely untouched, as angelic as the day Mohr first set eyes on her.

He turned to Pelz. 'Disable the booby trap and remove Major Weimann and the others for burial. Leave Frau Grabowski. Bring in wood from the store, make a pyre around her and then burn the dacha to the ground.'

Mohr turned and walked slowly from the dacha. Outside, a thin scattering of snowflakes was carried in the biting easterly wind, a herald from General Winter.

Squaring the Triangle

THE LARGE RECEPTION room seethed with people, their multiple conversations creating a wall of indistinct sound. The awards ceremony over, a crowd of dark-suited men and glamorously dressed women were now relaxed and circulating, wine glasses in hand. Colleagues, acquaintances and rivals mingled together, congratulations and commiserations being exchanged as required; a gathering of the great, the influential, the aspiring and the regionally famous.

But there was one exception: Alex Pentland stood by himself, half obscured beside a convenient fluted pillar. It was a position deliberately chosen, for he had soon wearied of this intensive post-ceremony socialising. He'd had his fill of catching up with old acquaintances and more than enough of talking with work colleagues, many of whom he had seen earlier that day at the studio. Alex believed his dislike of such events was perfectly reasonable. As a distinctly unglamorous business news reporter he had never been proposed for an award, could not believe he ever would be and rarely thought the winners particularly worthy. And behind all the congratulations and bonhomie, he always heard the same muttered professional jealousies. But even he was unsure whether his dislike of such events was a moral judgment on the perceived hypocrisy or a reflection of his own latent jealousy.

Peering round the pillar, he wondered where his wife might be. He was well aware that Sophie's attitude to this kind of gathering was diametrically opposed to his own. She loved the glitz and the glamour and the opportunity to renew old friendships. Even though she was not in view, he knew she would be at the heart of some group, busily making herself noticed if not actually networking. For it was no secret between them that she longed to get back to a significant presenting job in TV, the kind of role she'd had to abandon after the difficult birth and early years of their daughter, Flora. This was a period she had found – and was still finding – difficult, reconciling a mother's natural love for their daughter with an unexpected dead stop to her career.

Alex had to resort to his spectacles before he managed to locate her. She was in a group comprising three women and a man, and it was soon obvious that it was the man dominating the conversation. Because he was nearly a head taller than his audience, Alex was immediately struck by over-long brown hair swept back from a high, intelligent forehead. Barely under control, it somehow conveyed an immediate impression of cavalier independence, if not actual rebellion. Occasionally the man would restore any straying locks with a swift sweep of his hand, all without interrupting his discourse.

And whatever he was saying clearly held his small audience. Standing beside Sophie was her friend Lydia, but the third woman, younger and strikingly attractive, was not known to him. All three were paying close attention to the speaker, who occasionally emphasised a point with an incisive hand gesture.

As he watched, it soon became clear to Alex that Sophie's interest might be rather more than just polite attentiveness. In the occasional moments when her face was visible, he was surprised to see an expression of unconscious pleasure. He suddenly realised it was a long time since he had seen Sophie display anything like it. In her TV presenter heyday, it had been different. Then, when she had interviewed someone famous and attractive, he would sometimes discern a similar animation. But that was some years ago, before Flora's birth, and Alex could not recall such intensity in recent times. This unexpected revelation caused a frisson of excitement to run through his body like a minor electric shock, and there was no mistaking its principal location.

He had been inclined to track Sophie down and see if she was ready – or could be persuaded – to leave for their room. But now Alex postponed any such thought, his interest aroused by her unexpected behaviour. It took no persuasion for him to remain by the pillar and watch his wife's obvious enjoyment, and he would have been more than happy to continue his observations but another acquaintance presented himself. By the time he had moved on, Sophie's group had disappeared.

∽

'Hello, you must be Alex.' The unfamiliar voice came from behind, so that he had to turn around to identify the speaker. He was astonished to find himself looking into the smiling face of the long-haired cavalier.

'I'm Robert Furneaux.' He held out a hand, which Alex shook. 'Sophie told me where I'd find you. We've been having such an interesting talk that I got carried away and rather hogged her company. I hope you don't mind.'

'No, not at all.' Alex struggled to recover from his initial surprise. 'I could see she was heavily engaged, but she can be an enthusiastic talker so I hope you weren't too intimidated.'

'You're being very unkind,' Furneaux replied, laughing.

'She is absolutely charming. You're a lucky man, Alex, but I imagine you know that already. But it's as a result of our little discussion that I thought it might be helpful to have a word with you. I don't know whether you are familiar with my work at all?'

'I'm afraid not.'

'Sensible man.' Robert Furneaux knew when to use the common touch. 'I'm supposed to be some sort of academic, but that simply means I've been lucky enough to write a couple of books that proved popular. In turn, that allowed me to bluff my way into a university across the pond as a visiting professor. I'm probably best summarised as a bit of a fraud, but that doesn't alter the fact that I'm here on a short promotional tour. Sorry to burden you with tedious detail but it might help when I get to the point.'

He paused to give an easy grin, displaying a fine array of regular teeth in the process. 'Officially that's all I'm here for but there is an extra. My agent tells me we have interest in a film deal on my latest book, although that's rather confidential at the moment. And here's the point: if it comes off, I would like to have a pre-recorded interview ready for the publicity splurge. For that I need an experienced interviewer who can ask sensible questions but whose own ego won't get in the way. Although I've only met Sophie this evening, she seems eminently qualified to me.'

'Well, she's certainly an experienced interviewer, I can vouch for that,' said Alex, before considering another benefit. 'And she's a free agent at the moment, as I expect she told you.'

'She didn't dwell on it but I could see her work means a lot to her. If this deal comes off, I hope it would be good for both of us. I must be careful not to exaggerate the chances of this film deal – I've been there before and absolutely zilch happened. That's why I wanted to speak to you first.

Before I broach the subject in more detail with Sophie, I felt it best to ask if you can see any downsides or problems. I'm concerned not to cause any disappointment.' Although his manner projected a certain youthful enthusiasm, concern was evident in his tanned face while he paused for an answer. He stood easily, Alex noticed, rangy and fit like a recently retired athlete who keeps himself in good shape.

Alex considered for a moment. 'None that I can think of but you really need to speak to Sophie. I wouldn't dream of speaking for her; it would be more than my life was worth. She can be very independent minded.'

'Sure, I understand.' There were times when Robert's American influence showed itself, both in his expressions and his mid-Atlantic accent. 'That's good, because my work sometimes stirs up a bit of controversy from the more militant feminists – I'm sure you're aware of them – so it would help to have a strong-minded interviewer. I see this interview as lively, challenging, provocative even – but, of course, the key point is that it generates publicity. In fact, I'm rather banking on some controversy because there's really no such thing as bad publicity in the promotional world, if you know what I mean.'

'I think I do, yes.'

'Look, I'm afraid there are a number of people I can't avoid seeing tonight, so I ought to get back to the fray. I'll try to speak to Sophie again this evening though I can't be certain it will happen. But it would be great to get to know you both, while we have the chance. Have you taken a room here?'

'Yes, just for tonight. We'll be off first thing in the morning.'

'As will I. Let's make sure we meet up before either of us leaves. We could grab a quick breakfast or coffee, or something. What's your room number, Alex?'

They exchanged numbers and then Robert Furneaux,

self-appointed academic fraud, departed back to his fray, leaving a definitely bewildered Alex at his chosen observation post.

☙

It was by the same pillar that Sophie Pentland found her husband a few minutes later. 'Are you still avoiding everyone?' she asked breathlessly. She didn't wait for a reply before continuing, 'You'll never guess who I've been talking to.'

'Won't I?' said Alex, deadpan.

'Robert Furneaux, the writer and academic among numerous other things. He's here with his agent, Charlotte; very nice as well as stunningly beautiful. He certainly knows how to pick them. Feminists tend to hate him because his books have terribly controversial views about women juggling careers and family and trying to have it all. He's very easy to talk to, not at all confrontational. There was also a hint of possible work for an interviewer, so you can imagine my ears pricked up at that. He asked about you as well, although I wasn't sure whether he was just being polite. I said you were probably hiding and he liked that idea. Said you were a man after his own heart and asked where you were. Lydia was really taken with him, and made it a bit obvious, but that's nothing new. I told her afterwards she needed to go and take a cold shower.'

It occurred to Alex that Lydia might not be the only one to require a cold shower. Sophie's breathless litany left him in little doubt that his wife was equally taken with the man, and he was curious whether she was aware of it. Before their one-sided conversation could resume, Alex saw the alleged agent, Charlotte, weaving towards them through the crowd.

'Hello again, Sophie. And you must be Alex.'

Viewed close to, Charlotte's loveliness was not one whit diminished. Alex felt the full force of her vivid blue eyes as she introduced herself and shook his hand. She smiled as she did so, but he thought it a shade mechanical, the smile of a professional required to be pleasant. Perhaps she was just tired or, like him, simply bored by an evening that held little interest for her.

Charlotte turned her attention to Sophie. 'As Robert hinted earlier, there's a chance that he might require an experienced interviewer in the near future. He's busy at the moment but he wondered whether you would be willing to discuss the possibility later this evening. We could meet in his room where it will be quiet. I'll be there to fill in any background you need to know. Robert's not always good on that sort of detail.'

Overcoming her surprise, Sophie managed a nod of assent and a husky, 'Yes, I don't see why not.'

Charlotte switched her gaze back to Alex. 'You're welcome to come, Alex, but I'm afraid it will be a rather dry meeting. After an evening of this' – she made a sweeping gesture towards the still-crowded room – 'we would quite understand if you preferred to relax in your own room.'

For a moment he wasn't sure whether he was being deliberately discouraged, but decided it was merely polite consideration. He looked at Sophie. 'I'm not sure you need me there. You've always organised your own business perfectly well, but I'll come if you want me to.'

Sophie frowned. 'Well, it's been a long evening, particularly for you. I know how you dislike these affairs. I don't suppose it will be a long meeting, will it, Charlotte?'

'No, I'm sure it won't be.'

'Then I'm sure I can manage on my own.'

'Good. Shall we say eleven o'clock? It's on the sixth floor, room eighteen. We look forward to seeing you then.' With a brisk goodnight to Alex, Charlotte turned and headed back into the crowd, an undulating locomotion displaying yet another of her notable assets.

Sophie exhaled a long breath through pursed lips and looked at her husband. 'Well, what about that? Robert Furneaux wants to see me about some possible work. I didn't imagine for one moment tonight would come up with that.'

'No, it's certainly out of the blue – but all the better for it. You deserve a break, Sophie, so let's hope something comes of it.' He consulted his watch. 'Look, it's nearly ten thirty. I think we should go back to our room so you have a chance to freshen up before this meeting. And you can plan your negotiating strategy.'

❧

Despite his tiredness, Alex could not asleep. The bed was comfortable enough but he was both fidgety and too hot. That was the trouble with these modern hotel rooms: utterly indistinguishable, too warm and usually stuffy, as if the hoteliers feared claims for compensation if a breath of fresh air found its way in. He looked at the illuminated bedside clock. Nearly a quarter past midnight. Where was his wretched wife? It was only supposed to be a short meeting. On the other hand, when Sophie was enthused about something, she could chat for England.

Alex had been aware of Sophie's suppressed excitement as she freshened up. She had renewed her make-up with great care but not changed her clothes. That was hardly surprising because, earlier in the evening, he had watched with some amusement as she wriggled into a shade-too-small dress, a process that had taken a minute or two of vigorous convulsions. Although blessed with an excellent figure Sophie put on weight easily, as he had mentioned undiplomatically during her struggle. But the result was certainly eye-catching, making no great demands on the imagination of any interested viewer. Years ago he had overheard a comment about Sophie's figure between a couple of work colleagues: 'pneumatic' was the word used, and it had stuck with him for, in certain dress styles, it was not difficult to imagine she had been somehow extra-inflated.

His sleepless mind expanded its considerations. Could Sophie really be smitten with this man Furneaux? Apparently he was quite famous in his field, whatever that might be. He certainly wasn't famous with Alex but he was a business reporter, not a job that required him to display a deep knowledge of the intricacies of the female psyche. He'd interviewed a fair number of women CEOs and entrepreneurs in his time, interesting enough but still just work. Now this man had suddenly appeared out of nowhere and Sophie was exhibiting an unusually keen interest. Furneaux might be a total blank with Alex but apparently not with a certain stratum of intelligent women, and Alex found it only too easy to see why they might find him attractive.

And now Sophie and Furneaux were ensconced in the man's room, supposedly talking about some vague business proposition that might never happen. The additional presence of the agent, Charlotte, provided some reassurance but even so… In this agitated state of mind, it suddenly occurred to Alex whether reassurance as to his wife's fidelity was actually what he wanted. He found her interest in Furneaux strangely fascinating. He was aware of an extraordinary paradox: the thought of them having sex together was simultaneously disturbing and arousing.

The door opened and he heard Sophie enter the room. The blue night light provided adequate illumination for her to enter the en-suite bathroom, where Alex heard muted sounds of preparation for bed. At length he heard the en-suite door open and felt Sophie slide into the bed beside him. For no discernible reason he pretended to be sleep.

An indeterminate time later, when he was actually on the threshold of sleep, he felt Sophie's leg brush against his own. It was a sign he knew well. He turned over to face the indistinct figure beside him and was immediately engulfed in a flood of passion. Sophie led the way in a rare display of initiative, in turn stimulating Alex into a sustained performance that he thought had long since deserted him. But even in the midst of their urgent, breathless love-making, he could not help wondering just who Sophie imagined she was having sex with.

❧

In the morning, much earlier than Alex would have liked, he heard Sophie asking if he was awake before immediately going on to say they were to meet Robert for breakfast in half an hour. Squinting at the clock, he was not impressed to find it was only seven fifteen.

'Why so early?' he protested.

'Because he's got to be away by nine o'clock.'

'And we've got to suffer for it?' responded Alex, only half in jest.

'Robert wants to meet you properly this time, so don't be grumpy. Just be your usual charming self.'

'After last night I'm not sure I've got the energy to be charming.'

She gave a guileless smile. 'Yes, awards ceremonies are exhausting, aren't they?'

❧

If Sophie and Alex arrived at the appointed time, Robert Furneaux did not. A waiter came and offered a telephoned apology for the delay, but minutes continued to tick by without his appearance. Alex, not inclined to wait for company to arrive, tucked into a full English breakfast.

Sophie settled for a croissant and coffee, but became noticeably impatient as time dragged on.

Robert arrived with a flourish, progressing across the dining room with long, loping strides, avoiding intervening tables with athletic agility. Apologies were swift and profuse. 'Modern technology – where would we be without it? But hell, it plays havoc with your schedule. I've left Charlotte to deal with the lesser queries, so I'm afraid she won't be able to join us, poor girl. But, hey, it was great last night, wasn't it?'

And so it goes on, thought Alex. A one-sided conversation that draws everybody in – but only to the extent that Robert Furneaux is willing to permit. He delved into Alex's job, 'sounds fascinating', their daughter Flora, 'must be tremendously fulfilling', and, more bizarrely, the absurd property prices in London. He spoke less to Sophie than Alex, as if making up for detaining her longer than anticipated the previous evening. And then, suddenly, it was time to go.

"Fraid I'm going to have to tear myself away from your company but, look, here's an idea. A friend of mine gives me free run of his holiday cottage on the Suffolk coast at Aldeburgh. You may know it. Anyway, I'm going there this weekend, Friday night through to Sunday morning. Charlotte will be there, too. It would be great if you guys could join us. You know, nothing strenuous, just eating out and going to the beach, chilling out in general. There's a chance we'll know more about this film deal by then. If so, it would be an opportunity to bring you up to speed on that. What do you say?'

Sophie and Alex looked at each other. There was no chance for discussion, so Alex could only say, 'Well, I'm not on the rota for the weekend bulletins but what about a baby-sitter? Your mother has already had Flora for two nights recently. Isn't it a bit much to ask her again so soon?'

'Oh, you know she loves looking after her,' responded Sophie, a shade swiftly, Alex thought.

'Then it's a date,' said Robert, disposing of any doubt. 'I'll get Charlotte to forward all the details.'

֍

When he was gone, Alex leaned back in his chair. 'The whirlwind has passed. Normal service is now resumed.'

Sophie smiled wryly. 'Come on, he just takes a bit of getting used to, that's all. And it's really good of him to invite us for the weekend. I can't remember when we last did anything like that. It should be fun, the four of us.'

'I noticed you didn't hesitate to commit your mother.'

'Well, you know what she's like with Flora. She won't mind and nor will Dad, if it comes to that. They'll be perfectly happy to look after her.'

'If you say so, Sophie; they're your parents. We didn't get much chance to discuss it, though, did we? There seemed to be a strong element of presumption about it.'

'Are you saying you don't want to go?'

He thought for a moment. 'No, I'm not saying that. I think I mean we really don't know the man, and it feels as though we are being swept along by some sort of human hurricane. And I'm presuming that his relationship with the alleged agent, Charlotte, is based on the old uncle-niece subterfuge, although I can't say I blame him for that.'

'I don't think she is actually the agent, more the agent's representative. She seems to double as a personal assistant while he's in the UK.' Sophie cocked her head on one side in puzzlement. 'As for being his "niece", as you so delicately put it, I was surprised to find she had her own room here. Like you, I had rather assumed…'

'That might just be for appearances.'

'I hardly think people bother about that sort of thing now, Alex. Or are you just kidding me, as usual.'

'I couldn't possibly say.' He looked at his wife with studied solemnity. 'Anyway, it looks as though we've been corralled into visiting Aldeburgh next weekend. Let's hope both the weather and the company prove congenial. There could well be something in it for you and, at the very least, that should make it worthwhile. Let's hope so.'

※

Three days later, Alex and Sophie were bound up in traffic on the M25, even though they had left early to try and avoid the rush hour. The A12 route to the Suffolk coast was not one they knew well but the traffic thinned noticeably as Chelmsford and Colchester passed into the rear-view mirror. Crossing Dedham Vale, the low September sun picked out the dusty autumn colours on the trees and threw their long shadows across the fields in dark counterpoint. A hare picked its way across the stubble only yards from the road, a denizen of another world. In the bucolic beauty of Constable Country, London seemed very far away.

In spite of satnav, they only found the cottage after much fruitless searching. Two false sightings and a couple of dead-ends had eventually persuaded them to stop and ask a dog walker. She knew the property, more pertinently that it was hidden behind a dense shrubbery and displayed no visible house name. As if it were trying to deter visitors, she added.

Two cars parked in the ample gravelled space beside the building indicated that Robert and Charlotte had already arrived. Overlooking the drive was a substantial old building, a half-timbered, pantiled house of the kind originally favoured by prosperous yeoman farmers. As they drew to a halt, Alex remarked that if this were the owner's humble holiday cottage, he'd be fascinated to see his main residence.

Their approach must have been heard because, as Sophie

switched off the car engine, Robert appeared at the door. He greeted them with the same boyish enthusiasm Alex had noted on their first acquaintance and, despite the new arrivals' protests, insisted on carrying both their weekend cases into the house. Their room was large for a bedroom, but modestly furnished with old stripped-pine bedside chests, drawers and wardrobe. But the bed was fitted with a modern mahogany headboard that did not match the other furniture and gave an impression of making do.

Returning downstairs, they were re-introduced to Charlotte, now more casually dressed in jeans and sweater but, to Alex's eyes, just as elegant. Her greeting was warm enough but hardly enthusiastic, as though she had passed up a more attractive country-house weekend to be there.

Robert, for whom enthusiasm was second nature, immediately took charge and explained the evening's arrangements. They would eat out at a restaurant he knew well; he could guarantee the food would be first class. And obviously it would be sensible for them all to travel in one vehicle, Robert's spacious SUV being ideal.

This good-humoured organisation reminded Alex of a tour guide he and Sophie had encountered once during a holiday in Greece; his service was impossible to fault but its very perfection generated a guilty sense of irritation. There was no denying the quality of the restaurant's meal, however, and the conversation flowed ever more easily as the courses passed and the wine flowed. Even the enigmatic Charlotte entered into the spirit with a dry wit that proved a measured counterfoil to Robert's more hearty humour. At his insistence the bill was paid by Robert, but he deflected any possibility of annoying Alex by suggesting he fund a substantial tip. Thus were good relations preserved.

It was completely dark by the time they left the restaurant and made their way back to the car. As they reached the vehicle, unmissable in a sudden array of flashing lights, Robert stopped at the driver's door and turned to Charlotte. 'I suppose you're going to say I shouldn't drive in my inebriated condition.'

'Quite right. You've drunk more than any of us.' She sounded briskly censorious.

'All right, you drive then. Here are the keys.' He handed them to the disapproving Charlotte before continuing, 'And so that I don't contaminate you with my alcoholic breath, I'm going to sit in the back. That means Alex will have to sit next to you, just to maintain the man-woman balance so favoured in our gender-equal society. Watch out though, Alex, she can be a terror when roused.'

'Be quiet, Robert, and get in the car.' In the darkness it was hard to tell whether Charlotte was annoyed or amused. As they sorted themselves into the revised seating arrangements, Robert leaned over to Sophie and whispered, 'I'm not really drunk, I just like to wind her up occasionally. But I also wanted to sit next to you.'

Charlotte started the car. 'Stop whispering in Sophie's ear, Robert. It's very bad manners.'

The return journey was relatively uneventful, although Robert sat closer to Sophie than was strictly necessary, occasionally stage-whispering disparaging comments about Charlotte's driving. Back at the cottage, Charlotte made coffee while Sophie phoned her parents and the two men engaged in a conversation about the merits of various restaurants they had visited. Although their gastronomic experiences were not so different, it came as no surprise to Alex that their dining companions differed markedly. Robert's roll call of the rich and famous hardly bore comparison, so Alex was not sorry when phone calls and coffees were finished and Sophie announced she was ready for bed. Charlotte immediately echoed this sentiment and the two women left together.

The departure of the women did not prompt Robert to follow suit, causing Alex to hesitate before heading for bed himself. Instead Robert lapsed into a reflective mood, rolling his whisky around in the glass and studying it as though it were an object of great fascination.

'You know, Alex, we're a lucky pair, out this evening with two beautiful women on our arms. Did you notice all the male eyes in the restaurant taking in the view? You could see them thinking how lucky we were, their envy rising up like a miasma. I suppose it's quite understandable. I'm guilty of it myself from time to time.' He smiled fondly at his glass and then glanced at Alex. 'Do you ever get fed up with men ogling Sophie? I mean, you know exactly what's going through their minds.'

'I don't give it much thought, Robert.'

'Really? But you must be aware of it.'

'Yes, I suppose I am but it goes with the territory, if you know what I mean. After all, Sophie was a well-known presenter for several years, and any woman in that position gets noticed – if not always for the right reasons. We're both used to it, but it's nowhere near as intensive as it used to be. We're older now and I think that probably makes us view it differently.'

'Ageing, yes. It comes to us all, Alex. How old are you, if I may ask?'

Alex smiled a shade ruefully. 'I won't see a three in front of my age again. Sophie's younger; she's thirty-eight, but don't tell her I said so.'

'And how long have you been married?'

'Ten years, eleven in a couple of months' time. We left it a while before having Flora because of Sophie's career. But that's the trend these days, isn't it?'

'Nearly eleven years, that's impressive. My marriage didn't last half that. And I left it a long while before getting hitched, you know, hoping some maturity might develop. A fond hope but ultimately futile. I'm pretty sure success in my career hastened the end of my marriage. Long separations and a much-changed lifestyle – it was as if it were destined to end unhappily and it did.' Robert added an apparently throwaway line. 'You've survived the seven-year itch, anyway. I doubt I could have managed that. Certainly not with some of the offers I've had.'

Alex walked into the trap. 'Ah, are those the sort of offers that it would be ungentlemanly to refuse?'

'You'd be amazed, Alex. Please don't think I'm boasting or exaggerating, but it really is a hazard of my job. Notes pushed into my hand, phone numbers, text messages, invitations to hotel rooms or even their homes. More bizarrely, I've even had approaches from supposedly arch-feminists who, half an hour before, were excoriating my books on some TV chat show.' Robert laughed, as if he found this particularly appealing. 'But if that's strange, I'll tell you what I find oddest of all. It's husbands who make the approach on behalf of their wives. It's more common than you might believe. Some do it at their wives' prompting; others want it to be a surprise, a kind of gift or present. They seem to have reached a stage in their marriage where they are absolutely sure of each other but want an extra stimulus in their lives. And why not, if it helps keep their relationship fresh? Sometimes I've even been pleased to help out.'

He was smiling during this let's-all-be-adults-about-this revelation but all the while scrutinising Alex's face for any discernible reaction.

'Sounds like a good deal for you, Robert.'

'Well, it certainly adds an interesting new dimension. I view it as a kind of human equilateral triangle: there are three equal parties, all of whom get what they want.' He studied Alex thoughtfully. 'If I may ask, have you ever considered anything like that to help preserve that vital spark in your marriage?'

'Is that the drink asking?' enquired Alex, poker faced. 'But anyway, the answer is no.'

'Don't be offended, Alex. It's just that you don't seem to mind my interest in Sophie or her interest in me. On the contrary, you seem quite fascinated by our relationship, and that fascination certainly doesn't seem to be driven by jealousy. If it were, I can't imagine you would have come on this weekend. And you would probably have reacted differently to Sophie staying late in my room at the hotel, or to my behaviour in the car tonight. Forgive my psychology training, but I see you watching Sophie and enjoying her pleasure in my company. Perhaps you even find it exciting.'

'I think you're barking up completely the wrong tree, Robert.'

'Possibly, it has been known. But I don't think so. Let me ask you one simple question to illustrate my point. Since the awards evening, has your sex life taken a distinct turn for the better?'

'I think that's more than enough of this conversation, Robert. I'm off to bed.'

'Please don't be offended, Alex. I'm just following my instincts and training. But if, on reflection, you find a certain prospect has some appeal, why not broach the subject with Sophie? It would be interesting to hear what she says.'

~

Sophie was already in bed but not asleep when Alex entered their room. The bedroom lacked an en-suite but a corner unit housed a wash basin where he washed his hands and cleaned his teeth. As he changed for bed, Sophie commented, 'You don't seem to have much to say. I thought you would be full of what you'd talked about with

Robert. I take it you are still speaking.'

'Oh, yes, I think you can say we are definitely speaking.'

'What do you mean by that? You haven't fallen out, have you?'

'No, no.' Alex frowned, as if considering that possibility. 'No, we are certainly speaking, although I find with Robert that some of his utterances are, shall we say, rather direct.'

It was Sophie's turn to frown. 'Whatever do you mean?'

'He's spent the last quarter of an hour explaining how women are a hazard in his work. You know, offers that he can't refuse.' Alex was careful to avoid specifics. 'Fortunately I only got the broad picture, not the intimate detail.'

'Sounds like typical man talk to me, or rather boys boasting about their conquests.'

'No, it wasn't like that. He was almost humble about it.'

'I suppose it's not surprising when you think of his lifestyle. After all, he's escorted Hollywood actresses to film festivals. Maybe not your front-rank stars but some well-known names, even so. A man like that is bound to attract some attention. I did tell you he was quite famous in his own way.'

'OK, if you put it like that.' He hesitated, wondering whether to continue. 'Just out of interest, does he do anything for you?'

'Alex Pentland, is this the green-eyed monster I see before me?' Sophie smiled, playing the coquette.

'Well, he certainly fancies you. I just wondered if it's mutual.'

'Are you serious?' She felt it safest to answer a question with a question. 'What makes you think he fancies me? I can't imagine he's actually told you.'

'Not explicitly, but anyone can see he's not blind to your charms.'

'Anyone can see those. They're difficult to hide.'

'You're just being flippant now.' Ready for bed, he

climbed in.

'All right, since you asked. Yes, of course I'm aware of some interest but it's hardly something new, is it? And I've always thought you coped really well with that sort of thing.'

'I'm not sure it's ever been quite so high powered.'

'It's all the same to me.'

Alex turned off the bedside lamp and decided to take a risk. 'Are you sure? Think back over these last few days. When did we last have sex like that?'

'For God's sake, Alex, where are you going with this? What on earth has our sex life got to do with Robert Furneaux?'

'Oh, come on, Sophie. Don't be disingenuous. It's as if a button has been pushed for both of us.'

There was brief silence in the darkness before she answered. 'I don't know what you expect me to say to that.'

'I'm not angry or upset or anything, not at all. It's just, well, noticeable, if you know what I mean. And it's been good as far as I'm concerned, I can assure you. I'm simply interested to know if it's been as good for you.'

'I'm not entirely happy with this conversation but I suppose it's possible there's something in what you say. A lot of women find him attractive; why should I be any different? It doesn't necessarily mean I want to jump into bed with him.'

Alex pressed on, totally uncertain how this would end. 'But hypothetically, if circumstances permitted and I didn't exist or object, would you like to have sex with Robert?'

'But you do exist and would surely object.'

There was a longish silence before Alex took the plunge. 'I'm not entirely sure I would, Sophie. If it was what you really wanted, I'm not sure I would object. He's hardly a threat to our marriage, is he? Abroad most of the time or jetting around the world. I can't see you running after that.'

In the darkness it was impossible to see Sophie's reaction. Another long silence played on his doubts about the wisdom of the conversation. 'Are you still there?'

'Well, I haven't run off to Robert's bedroom, if that's what you're thinking. But you have surprised me, Alex. More than surprise – I'm amazed. I can hardly believe it's you talking.'

'Perhaps I'm more surprising than you think.'

'You can say that again. And I had you down as Mr Conventional.'

'Yes, I know.' Relieved to have avoided an angry reaction, he determined to press on. 'But maybe it would be a good thing to break out of our routine occasionally, just for a change. As long as we both agree, of course.'

'I don't know, Alex. An occasional surprise is one thing but what you seem to be talking about would be a huge step, for me at least.' She hesitated for a moment before adding, 'And I'm struggling to see what you get out of it.'

'I know it must seem odd. Ten years ago I wouldn't have dreamed of it, but we become different people every ten years, so they say.' Alex preferred not to have his own motives examined too closely. 'Do you remember Ewan and Amanda? Best of friends and all that, until it became clear they were very keen for us to swap partners. We just laughed about it at the time.'

Sophie was not so easily distracted. 'Yes, I remember very well. But that was then and this is now. And I want to be absolutely clear, Alex: are you really saying that if I want to have sex with Robert Furneaux, you would approve?'

'I don't think approve is the right word but, if it was what you really wanted, I'm not sure I would object.'

'That's not exactly a ringing endorsement, is it? Are you sure you know what you're saying? And would it be sensible, for either of us?'

'We're supposed to be grown-ups, Sophie. Surely we can talk about these things and decide for ourselves. Of course it's not the sort of topic we'd discuss with the neighbours, or even friends. Only we would know. It's nobody else's business and that is definitely how we should keep it.'

There was another hiatus until Sophie broke the silence. 'Well, what an evening this has turned out to be. My husband, the sexual adventurer: not a moniker I ever thought would apply to you, Alex. And I'm certainly not sure that what you're suggesting is at all wise. I still don't understand your motive. Or have you a girlfriend in mind that you want to shag? And this would clear the way?'

'You must be joking. Chance would be a fine thing. You're reading too much into my side of this, Sophie. I don't want it to sound like altruism but, honestly, I think I'd be happy if you were happy. There's nothing more to it than that. Something has spiced up our love life and if a little adventure on your part maintains that, then I may well go along with it.'

'I see – or rather I'm not at all sure that I do. You're the one who's talked about a whirlwind sweeping into our lives, and now I beginning to see what you mean. It's certainly unsettling and it might even be, oh I don't know, risky somehow, to our relationship. Anyway, I've had more than enough surprises for one night. I want to get to sleep, so goodnight.'

It was a sure sign of Sophie's unsettled state of mind that she failed to kiss him.

ঔ

Alex slept fitfully, surfacing several times during the night before falling asleep heavily as the dawn light began to show through the curtains. As a consequence, he woke late, unrested and with a thick head. Sophie was missing until he found her downstairs with Charlotte. They had already eaten a minimal breakfast and were now chatting over coffee. He was surprised to notice that, without make-up, Charlotte's looks appeared much less striking, almost as though she were a different woman. An unfair observation, he thought, as Sophie was no different but he was used to her.

As for Sophie, she appeared to be in good spirits, informing Alex that she and Charlotte were going to tour Aldeburgh's shops during the morning. He and Robert would have to amuse themselves. It was not a prospect that filled Alex with much joy but that was to be the arrangement because, it transpired, Charlotte was leaving immediately after lunch and this would be the only opportunity for the two women to spend time together doing what they wanted. Faced with a united front, Alex bowed to superior forces with reasonably good grace.

It was gone ten before Robert put in an appearance, by which time the women had left for the shops. He had been catching up on some urgent work, or so he claimed. Alex was inclined to think he had been having a lie-in. It was past eleven by the time Robert had breakfasted and they agreed to embark on a bracing seaside walk.

Aldeburgh possesses a typical East Anglian coastline: a flat, marshy hinterland jutting into an often hostile North Sea like a boxer leading with his chin. In the weekend's quiet weather they saw only a subdued grey-green sea washing gently against the deep, shingle beach. Dragged high above the tideline, a few inshore fishing boats projected the illusory romance of the sea, the last survivors of a once-vital way of life. The stark shape of Maggi Hambling's giant sculpted scallop caught their attention, as controversial between the two of them as between the town's inhabitants.

As their walk progressed, Alex was relieved to find Robert an agreeable companion, lively in his observations without being overbearing. He also noticed that Robert coped much better with the strenuous walking over the shingle, so was thankful when they left the beach for a path through the marshes. A hazy sun tried to burn through the translucent high cloud but succeeded only intermittently, briefly bathing the fields and reedbeds in the soft light of early autumn. Endeavouring to complete a circular route, it was only as they began the last mile of their walk that Robert raised a subject not connected to their stroll.

'I hope you'll forgive my curiosity, Alex, but have you found an opportunity to speak to Sophie?' He didn't need to specify the subject.

Although the enquiry was not unexpected, Alex had still not resolved his frustrating dilemma. He was only too well aware that if he said yes, it would be an irrevocable admission that he had considered the proposal and approved of it, thereby confirming all Robert's infuriating presumptions. But if he said no, it would shut the door on a possibility that excited him more than he cared to admit. Such is the nature of dilemmas.

Not receiving an immediate reply, Robert declined to break the silence, understanding perfectly that Alex was on the verge of a crucial decision.

'Yes,' said a voice, and Alex had the distinct impression someone else had spoken. But he went on to add, 'Yes, I did mention it, the general gist. She was very surprised, a bit shocked actually, so I've very little idea how it went down. She didn't rant and rave but she didn't show any enthusiasm, which perhaps isn't surprising. The idea seemed to leave her distinctly underwhelmed, understandably so because it's well outside her comfort zone.'

'But she didn't rule it out,' probed Robert, very cautiously. 'She's actually thinking about it?'

'Well, I hardly saw her to speak to this morning, so it's

possible, I suppose. But judging by her reaction so far, I'll be surprised if she follows it up.'

'There's time yet. Let's see how things stand this afternoon. Charlotte's departure will remove a major distraction and then perhaps we'll get a clearer indication, or even an answer.' There seemed to be an assumption on Robert's part that they were now allies in a joint cause.

'Yes, that seems sensible.' Alex felt obliged to enter a note of caution. 'I wouldn't try to put any pressure on Sophie, you understand. Any decision must be entirely hers.'

'Of course, Alex, I wouldn't dream of it. I'm sure it would be completely counter-productive. Sophie's far too intelligent to be persuaded by any sort of conspiracy that we might be tempted to dream up. No, let's see how things play out as the day goes on. We're here for a relaxing weekend, so that should be our main priority.'

Alex heard this, but was not at all convinced. Conversation lapsed as they continued the final leg of their walk, each withdrawing into his own thoughts. With every step Alex became ever more acutely aware that he had now committed himself to a prospect about which he was still deeply ambivalent. Furthermore, it was disturbing to discover that, in a straightforward choice between risk and safety, he had opted for risk. Or was it excitement over staidness? He wasn't at all sure. He only knew that he had crossed some kind of arbitrary threshold and had no idea how it would end.

※

Charlotte departed immediately after lunch. As she said her goodbyes she was a schoolmistress to Robert, reminding him of people to contact, work to be delivered and schedules to be kept, all of which he took in good part. Warmly polite to Alex, she said that she had enjoyed his company and hoped they would meet again. To Sophie she displayed what seemed to be genuine affection, saying how she'd loved their shopping trip and they must do it again. She wished Sophie good luck; Alex wasn't sure whether this referred to the chance of work with Robert or the resumption of her career, or both. He also noted that Charlotte managed to climb into her low-slung Mini Cooper with elegant accomplishment.

The remaining trio spent the rest of the afternoon visiting the town's art galleries and studios, of which there appeared to be no shortage. Examples of every art form were on display, from polished stones taken from the beach to high-end paintings and sculptures. Robert persuaded himself to buy a small charcoal sketch of a ballet dancer which, however well it captured the grace and fluidity of her movement, made both Sophie and Alex wince inwardly at the price. It took a pot of tea for them to recover.

During their unhurried wanderings, Alex had ample opportunity to observe the interaction between Robert and Sophie. He had to admit that, for a man who admitted lusting after his wife, Robert disguised it well; he was attentive, engaging, amusing and charming, but nothing to excess. There were no calculated allusions or anything that could be construed as even mildly suggestive. Sophie was equally difficult to read as she made her own contribution of bright, cheerful conversation. Any casual observer, Alex thought, would have found it difficult to detect much in the way of sexual undercurrent between Robert and Sophie. At some moments, he found it difficult to believe in it himself.

It was only when they had returned to the house that Robert showed any sign of concern. While Sophie was in the kitchen checking on what was available for a simple evening meal, Robert took Alex's arm and steered him to the far end of the living room.

'Look, Alex, you'll have to help me out here because I'm a little confused.' His voice was much quieter than usual. 'Just to be clear about where we are, you understand. In summary, you know I'm greatly attracted to Sophie and would regard it as a huge privilege to sleep with her. You have considered that possibility and seem to agree. We both think Sophie also finds the idea agreeable, at least in the abstract sense. You've spoken about it and, importantly, she has not dismissed it out of hand. Nor has she reacted badly – this afternoon seems proof of that. So here's my difficulty, Alex: we seem to be three people who want the same thing but are somehow stuck. We need to find a way of squaring the triangle. You know Sophie better than anyone. What do you suggest?'

'Just a minute, Robert. I'm not Sophie's keeper. She must make up her own mind on this and I certainly won't put any pressure on her. That's what we agreed earlier.'

'Of course, I understand completely.' Robert's taut voice betrayed a touch of frustration. 'It's just that we don't have unlimited time. We'll be away first thing tomorrow morning and we have no idea when we might be able to meet up again. Busy lives and all that. This weekend is an opportunity that could be difficult to replicate. Is there nothing you can think of saying to Sophie that might nudge things along?'

Stifling a sense of irritation, Alex considered the request. 'Nothing definite springs to mind, Robert, but if a suitable opportunity arises, I'll see what I can do. If not, I'm afraid we'll both have to assume it's a non-runner with Sophie and that's that.'

'Well, I'm guided by you, Alex. You're the one who should know, or rather is in the position to find out. I leave it in your hands.' His flat tone suggested disappointment, an implied rebuke that he thought Alex might have undertaken to do more.

☙

The meagre selection of tins and packets did not lend themselves to a choice meal, despite Sophie's willingness to 'cobble something together'. They decided to telephone for pizzas, which were eventually delivered late due to difficulty in finding the cottage. After the meal it was a choice of board games or a DVD. Neither Alex nor Sophie had any particular preference so Robert chose for them, the epic romantic film Doctor Zhivago. As tends to be the way with films of Russian novels, the complicated love story of Lara Antipova and the eponymous doctor ran for three hours, extended only a little by a pause to make coffee. At its eventual conclusion Sophie, who had spent the entire film reclining decorously on the sofa, announced that she was ready for bed.

There was a lengthy silence after her departure. Robert gazed pensively into the unlit fireplace as if trying to ascertain its purpose. Alex sat a shade uncomfortably, wondering whether it would look rude if he immediately followed Sophie up to bed without further conversation. Robert eventually solved this dilemma and came straight to the point. 'Have you managed to speak to Sophie, by any chance?'

'I'm afraid not. As you know, we've been occupied with other things the whole evening and there simply hasn't been a chance.' He wasn't inclined to shoulder all the blame. 'I'd forgotten how long that film was.'

'Yes, that's true. We should have been warned by the word "epic", I suppose. Perhaps we should have watched Confessions of a Window Cleaner or something similar – short, sweet and not too taxing. If only it had been in the collection, it would have been my first choice.'

It was Robert's first attempt at humour that struck a jarring note, and Alex thought it almost certainly stemmed from disappointment. Unable to think of a suitable reply, he was saved the trouble by Robert adding, 'You know,

Alex, it's a sad fact of life that not all good things come to pass. It seemed as though there was an opportunity for each of us to get what we wanted but it looks as though it's an opportunity that's going begging this time. It's a pity, but not to worry.'

On this philosophical note, and to Alex's surprise, Robert rose from his armchair, grasped his hand and shook it, adding, 'Here's to better fortune next time.' Without elaborating further, he bade Alex goodnight and set off for bed.

For a few moments Alex stood and gathered his wits. He was, in truth, more than a little unsure whether he was relieved or disappointed. Over-riding these emotions was a sense of anti-climax, of regret that, having decided on an uncharacteristically bold, even reckless, course of action, it had come to nothing. With a shrug of his shoulders, he followed Robert up the stairs.

When he entered their bedroom, he found Sophie already in her dressing gown and in the last stages of preparing for bed. Having just finished cleaning her teeth, she sat down on the edge of the bed and looked expectantly at her husband. 'Have you been chatting to Robert?'

'Only briefly, and nothing of any great consequence. I think we exhausted most topics of conversation during the day.'

'Yes, I expect so.' She seemed keen to talk. 'I had a lovely time with Charlotte this morning, very useful, in fact. She's quite a girl, is our Charlotte, really got her head screwed on. She was very forthcoming about Robert, filling in various facets of his character and so on.'

'Oh yes, such as?'

'Well, you won't be surprised to hear he has a considerable ego but at least he attempts to hide it. Otherwise it seems he is very much as he appears: clever, easy-going, charming, likes women.'

'I could have told you that.'

'Yes, but it's nice to have it confirmed by one who knows. Much more importantly, Charlotte confirmed that his offer of interviewing work is genuine, although by no means guaranteed to come to anything.'

'Now you're talking. That is useful to know.' Alex started undressing for bed.

'Yes, I wasn't sure whether he might be stringing us along, you know, as a means to an end. But Charlotte was adamant that he wouldn't do such a thing, which was very reassuring. She also confirmed that he has a penchant for full-figure women, particularly if they are married.'

Alex stopped undressing and looked at his wife. 'She told you that?'

'Yes, she was quite open about it. But he likes to get the approval of the husband. It's his thing, apparently, as you have discovered.'

'My God, is she speaking from personal experience?'

'It seems Robert did come on to her – which is not at all surprising – and she told me she was certainly tempted. But, after much thought, she eventually declined the offer. She's a real character, that girl. And they've got on perfectly well ever since, so perhaps it was the right thing for her to do.'

'Wow, that was some girly chat you had.' Alex felt obliged to probe a little further. 'And I imagine you found that information quite useful in helping you to decide what you want to do?'

'Yes.' Sophie sounded quite definite. 'Of course, Charlotte had a good idea what Robert had in mind for this weekend, although she was diplomatic in speaking about it. I would have found it very disconcerting to discover that we'd become involved in a situation set up to fulfil the quirks of one man. Or rather, I would have thought that, if it hadn't been for your amazing revelation that you were willing to go along with it. That's taken some getting used to, I can tell you.'

Alex was hasty in his defence. 'Only if you wanted to. I left the decision entirely up to you. Anyway, I imagine it's academic now.'

'Really?' Sophie gave him a quizzical look. 'Why do you say that?'

It was Alex's turn to look perplexed. 'Well, I got the impression you had decided against the idea. You haven't said anything, or given the slightest indication that you were even considering it. I rather assumed…'

Sophie gave a mild frown. 'It's not something I would want to make too obvious. But talking with Charlotte cleared my mind of any doubts. I've decided to go ahead, while I've got the opportunity.'

Doubt clouded Alex's mind. 'Are we talking about the same thing here? Are you referring to the possibility of work or … the other thing?'

Sophie looked at her husband with calm directness. 'Both, if everything works out.'

'I see,' was all he could manage.

'I hope you're not changing your mind, Alex,' said Sophie, suddenly more serious. 'After all, we've only come to this point because of what you said. You offered me a choice, I've thought about it and I've decided to take it up.'

Alex struggled to cope with this unexpected turn, still mired in deep ambivalence. 'No, no. It's your decision entirely.' He remembered his last conversation with Robert. 'I think it will be a surprise to a certain individual.'

'Good. I wouldn't like to have appeared too eager. I wouldn't have felt comfortable with that.' She gave an impish smile. 'But I have gone to a little trouble on his behalf.'

Alex found speaking difficult. 'Oh, what's that?'

'While I was out shopping with Charlotte today, I bought

this.' Sophie stood up, undid the belt of the dressing gown and let it slip from her shoulders. Underneath was revealed a short black nightie with lace-thin straps and a low-cut top that only half-concealed her breasts. 'Charlotte told me he likes black. It's actually a slip rather than a nightie but it will have to do.'

Seeing her renewed excitement, Alex was beyond replying. Not noticing, Sophie continued, 'D'you know, I thought I'd be really nervous but, amazingly, I'm not. Well, perhaps just a bit. Anyway, here goes.' She gave him a peck on the cheek. 'I'll see you later.'

Frozen into silence, he could only watch as Sophie walked to the door, a vision in black indelibly imprinted on his scrambled brain. She closed the door quietly and without looking back.

~

On the landing, Sophie paused in the darkness. She had never felt this way before and wanted to savour the moment. Even now she could hardly believe it. A week ago she had been a humdrum housewife and mother, managing a family while struggling to resurrect some sort of career which, in her heart of hearts, she believed had passed her by. And now, in a whirlwind few days, she'd met a man who had rocked her world in a way she had almost forgotten. His interest in her had soon been obvious, and she couldn't deny the attraction was not only mutual but more powerful than she'd experienced in years. In fact, if Robert had come on to her in his hotel room on the awards night, she wasn't sure what the outcome would have been. She certainly hadn't told Alex that Charlotte had left after only ten minutes or so, and that she'd spent an hour alone in Robert's company. But then she had made a point of never admitting to her husband that, in her TV heyday, she had occasionally been tempted by some of the offers she had received. There were certain things a woman, particularly a wife, should always keep to herself.

As for Alex, he had been a revelation. With hindsight, perhaps his easy-going tolerance of other men's interest in her masked an inclination to voyeurism. And if that were true, why should she not also benefit? The reasoning seemed compelling. Sophie felt her way to Robert's bedroom door, took a deep breath and pushed down the handle.

～

As Robert gripped the heaving body beneath him and listened to Sophie's half-stifled moans, he wondered briefly about Alex. Was he still in his room, paralysed with regret or remorse? Or had he crept onto the landing and was even now crouched by the door, straining to hear his wife's ecstatic pleasure. He imagined the latter, spurring a renewed burst of energy to which Sophie immediately responded. He remembered his earlier analogy and smiled; the triangle had been squared

The Hidden Cost

THERE IS ALWAYS something to do, Arthur Dennison reflected. And the nature of his new work was such that it could never be finished, merely temporarily completed until its resumption the next day. But what some might regard as a disadvantage, Arthur relished, and would happily admit as much. Such were his idle thoughts as he made his way back to his home. Returning unexpectedly from cancelled appointments in town, he had left his car at the barn and put the time to good use by completing a few chores. Now a cup of tea would be welcome.

He followed the track as it wound its way through the wood, the trees clothed in a delicate green tracery of unfurling leaves, for the sap was rising strongly in the early April air. And it was through this hazy, green filigree that Arthur first glimpsed the house. At the edge of the track, his black Labrador picked up the scent of some passing creature – quite recently passed, if her keen interest was any guide. Normally Arthur would have noticed this immediately but his attention had been caught by something else.

To one side of the house was a lean-to woodstore and, beyond that, a long timber shed. In the space between, largely screened from any other viewpoint, was parked a vehicle. Arthur stopped. For several moments he stood and stared, too absorbed to register a woodpecker's strident drumming somewhere in the distance. Then he turned and spoke to the dog. 'Come on, Jess. Let's go and find another job.'

❧

Nearly three days elapsed before Rose found a suitable moment to raise the subject. During this time she had pondered, considered and speculated on every aspect of the proposition. Now, with the ironing almost finished and her husband settled into his favourite armchair, she decided it was time.

She spoke with studied casualness. 'There's a job advertised at the shop and I was wondering whether to apply for it.'

Arthur barely glanced up from his paper. 'Oh? I thought you'd had enough of shop work.'

'The card is in the shop window but it's not for shop work. It's book-keeping.'

This information gained a little more of his attention. 'You're getting ambitious in your old age, aren't you?'

'Well, it would be something different, that's for sure. But I quite like the idea, a change before I get too old, as you so graciously put it. I've got a qualification after doing those evening classes with Evelyn. And I looked after your various club accounts when you were too busy, all out of the goodness of my heart.'

'I gave you a box of chocolates occasionally.'

'Yes, paid for out of club funds, I expect.' Rose rested the iron on the asbestos pad and gave her husband a wry smile. 'Anyway, that's what I'm thinking.'

'And where would this be, assuming you were successful?'

'The Eastons' place, Manor Farm.' She wondered what reception this would provoke. It was immediate; suddenly Rose had his undivided attention.

'Is that so? Cameron Easton's place. That used to be one of our accounts. We used to supply and service all their equipment until they merged the farms, then Burroughs got it.' Arthur's brow furrowed in concentration. 'I'll tell you something else: I don't think the shooting is let. A fair bit of ground, too. There must be a thousand acres or more.'

'Well, I wouldn't be going there to get you more shooting, if that's what you're thinking.'

He grinned. 'No, I suppose not, although it would be nice. Bags of potential there.' Something else occurred to him. 'What's the state of play with their marriage now? Is she still living away?'

This was the enquiry Rose had anticipated. 'I'm not sure, but I think Caroline's still at her parents' with the children. There's always talk of her returning but it's not happened yet, as far as I know.'

'That was a rum do. Him getting involved with the nanny – and before that there were those rumours about that attractive young vet. Stupid really, the sort of thing you see on a TV drama.'

Rose hesitated for a moment. 'You don't think it should put me off applying, do you? You know, there's been a bit of a scandal and there's still plenty of talk.'

'What are you saying, that he might start chasing after you?' Arthur gave a rich laugh. 'Cor blast me, gal, yew hin't got t'worry on that score. Yer damn near old 'nuff ter be his mawther!'

Rose smiled dutifully. Arthur occasionally adopted this country-bumpkin voice, but she wished he wouldn't. It was rarely as amusing as he seemed to think. And, in this context, neither was it very flattering. She was certainly older than Cameron Easton but, at forty-six, she hardly felt ancient. Nor was she decrepit, being the epitome of a country girl, buxom and sturdy, with child-bearing hips and a round face that exuded good health from a rosy complexion, making her aptly named. But Arthur had never been one to make much of a fuss about her looks. And, at seven years older, he seemed to embrace comfortable middle age with enthusiasm where Rose nurtured a private grudge.

'That's all right, then. You won't be bothered by any scandalous gossip when I get this job.'

Arthur still thought it amusing. 'You get the job and then I'll worry about the gossip. You know what I think about village tittle-tattle: idle tongues, hinged in the middle so they can wag the more.'

Rose picked up the iron, content to let the conversation lapse. Her principal concern about applying had been dismissed comprehensively. All that remained now was the small matter of writing an application, obtaining an interview and getting the job.

~

Her application read better than she had dared hope but that was because Arthur helped her, him being used to dealing with job applications. Rose thought it looked quite impressive, until she considered who else might apply. There were many hidden talents locally, and this kind of role was much sought after in the limited world of village employment.

So it was with surprised delight that, a week later, she received a letter inviting her to an interview. Admittedly, the letter itself was not very professional; it was on headed paper certainly but handwritten, or, more accurately, scrawled in an untidy, florid hand. But there was no denying the content: Rose was to present herself for interview at ten thirty the following Tuesday.

It prompted an urgent bout of revision regarding book-keeping and, at Arthur's prompting, some discreet background research about Manor Farm's operations. 'It will give you something to talk about other than book-keeping, shows you've taken some trouble over your application. As long as you don't mention the trouble and strife.' There were times when Arthur could be quietly droll.

Indeed, after what had seemed to be initial scepticism, Arthur proved very supportive of Rose's application. Of course, she was aware Arthur had always been supportive, like any good husband. Whenever a major decision was required, whether it concerned moving home, a part-time job or a decision regarding the twins, Arthur always consulted her. There was even one occasion when, much against his own wishes, he had acceded to her preference.

This dated back to the time of their house move, twenty years ago. It was an episode that still puzzled Arthur, although it was a matter that had gradually slipped into the furthest recesses of his memory. They had been married four years by then and, thanks to Arthur's steady progression at the agricultural engineers where he worked, they had been able to afford a modest three-bed semi, even if the third bedroom did not permit the swinging of a cat.

He was still a young man then, with interests to match. Although football had passed him by, cricket was still on, as were darts and other pub-related activities. Arthur also had another abiding interest which took up considerable time: clay-pigeon shooting. This, along with many of his other activities, he shared with his great friend, Gerry. Although this friendship could not be described as inseparable, it was close and had endured since their teenage years. Naturally it had become more restricted after Arthur's marriage, but it had remained strong.

It was after the birth of the twins that Gerry came into his own. It is the nature of agricultural work that it is dictated by the seasons and, during harvest time, it is at its most demanding. If conditions are favourable, harvesting must go ahead into the night. Any machinery breakdowns require immediate attention, whatever the time of day or night. As the manager of an agricultural engineer's service department, it was Arthur's busiest time and no day, night or weekend was safe from callout. This was when Gerry had stepped into the breach. With Rose struggling with two babies only months old, Gerry had proved a rock, running shopping errands, cutting the grass and even coping with occasional domestic crises such as a malfunctioning washing machine. Both Arthur and Rose were deeply appreciative.

So it had come as a stunning shock to Arthur when Rose suddenly declared that she wanted to move. At the same time she had, almost overnight, become morose and edgy, which Arthur could only ascribe to some form of post-natal depression. But she would not see a doctor and had insisted she could now cope perfectly well with the twins.

With the harvest over, Arthur was at last able to spend more time at home and they had started to forge a new domestic routine, largely dictated by the infant twins. It had been no surprise to Arthur that Gerry's visits reduced, but he was surprised that they fell away to nothing. He assumed that Gerry, single and carefree, had experienced more than enough of domesticity over the previous three months.

Arthur had hoped that Rose's urge to move home would be forgotten in the demands of motherhood, but the opposite proved true. She insisted that the house was too small for a growing family, particularly the ridiculous third bedroom. That argument Arthur had understood; what he had not understood was Rose's insistence that they move from a village east of the town to one on the west side. True, Rose's parents lived in town and travelling to see them would hardly be affected, nor would his journey to work. But there was no escaping the fact that many of their friends would be left behind for no good reason that Arthur could discern.

There had been no let-up in Rose's insistence. If anything, it had become more strident, overlaid by a sense of unhappiness. So the new year had opened with Arthur collecting sheaves of property details, which they pored over, sifted and eventually reduced to a short-list of one. That had resulted in a move to the house they still occupied, now almost unrecognisable after Arthur undertook various improvements over the years, for he was a wonderfully versatile DIY man. And, he conceded, it had been a good move; they had made a new life for themselves and Rose was quickly restored to her usual good spirits. New friends and acquaintances soon followed, so Arthur's separation from Gerry quickly became a permanent break.

Now, with the twins having both left home, the house was larger than they actually needed. They were still comfortable there, so talk of moving again was almost non-existent. But in the rare, fleeting moments when Arthur thought back to their original move, Rose's insistence remained as much a mystery to him now as it had been twenty years earlier.

ൟ

When Arthur returned home from work on the day of Rose's interview, it was with a keener interest than he had anticipated. 'Well, how did it go?'

Rose pulled a wry face. 'Hard to tell. But I wasted my time researching farming because I wouldn't be involved in that side at all. It turns out he wants somebody to look after their property lettings. It seems they keep that business separate from the farm. He asked whether I knew anything about property and, of course, I had to say no. I couldn't even say we'd moved much. I was a bit put out really – I thought that ought to have been made clear in the ad.'

Arthur was less dispirited than Rose. 'It's the book-keeping part that's important and you should have been OK there.'

'Yes, that seemed to go down well enough.' Her spirits revived somewhat. 'He didn't make a big thing about the property side. It was more like background information, whether I thought I could cope.'

'And what did you say?'

'Well, after all that effort I was hardly going to say I was completely the wrong person for the job, was I? I fibbed through my teeth and said I thought I'd be fine.'

'That's my girl.' Arthur laughed gently. 'You gave the right answer there: confident and positive. That always goes down well.'

'Your name got a mention, by the way.'

'Did it?' He was immediately curious. 'I don't really know the man. We've only spoken a handful of times over the last dozen years, and then not specifically about business. I think the last time was at the county show a couple of years ago.'

Rose was quite definite. 'He knows of you, at least, and seemed quite impressed. Anyway, I don't think it did my prospects any harm. Now it's in the lap of the gods.'

~

The following day, the gods looked favourably upon Rose Dennison. Cameron Easton telephoned and offered the job to her and, after hearing the terms, she was pleased to accept. A start date was arranged for the following week; a letter of confirmation would follow shortly. If Rose was delighted, Arthur seemed equally pleased for her.

And so began Rose's employment at Manor Farm. The farm office being small and already cramped, Rose was found a room in a former outbuilding now incorporated into the house. It meant her contact with the other farm staff was quite restricted, particularly as she only worked two days a week. But it was not a handicap, since her work had no direct connection to the farm operations and her office was convenient if she needed to refer to Cameron. He proved diligent in helping Rose settle in and a regular visitor thereafter. Within a couple of months it was as if Rose had been there for years.

Arthur, well aware that new employment arrangements could be a testing time for both parties, was also happy that the arrangement was working out. He was pleased for Rose, of course, but there was another factor, as yet unspoken, for Arthur nurtured a secret aspiration. It concerned the sporting rights of Manor Farm, whether they were vacant and the chances of him securing them.

From the day he had first learnt of Rose's interest in the job and the name of her prospective employer, his interest had quickened. An idea had germinated in his head and, as the weeks passed, its roots spread and deepened with all the vigour of Japanese knotweed. It also proved as tenacious as that plant, defying all attempts to moderate its vaulting ambition.

At first, Arthur had simply consulted a large-scale Ordnance Survey map to remind himself of the farm's topography. Then, when Rose obtained an interview, he felt drawn to drive casually around the few lanes crossing the farm, stopping occasionally to familiarise himself in three-dimensional detail. When Rose's employment was confirmed, he had gone even further, slipping along the hedges and spinneys like a thief in the night. Arthur was not bent on theft, merely keen to check the coverts' suitability for holding pheasants.

In meditative moments, he would roll the names of the woods around in his head: the Larches; Abe's Folly; the Claypit; Doctor's Planting, names redolent of past sporting days that he would be only too willing to restore. In his mind's eye, Arthur could see the pheasants darkening the sky as they winged their way from one covert to the next. Over time he came to realise that, to attain such a vision, he would be prepared to make considerable sacrifices.

Arthur bided his time but when it became apparent Rose's employment at the farm was established, he decided to speak up. His opportunity arose when Rose finished recounting some minor event that had occurred during her morning's work.

'You seem to have settled in nicely. Happy in your work, that's the main thing.'

'Yes, I've got the hang of it now. It's really not that complicated, just needed a bit of getting used to. Cameron's been very good. I might have struggled if he hadn't taken such trouble to show me the ropes.' Rose smiled in affirmation. 'Yes, he's been very helpful.'

Arthur's question sounded innocuous enough. 'By the way, have you discovered if there is a sporting tenant on the farm? Has somebody got the shooting rights?'

Rose was sceptically amused. 'You're still angling after that, are you? I should have known.'

'Well, I just wondered whether it might fall under your wing, as well as the property side? You seem to deal with all the odds and ends, after all.'

'I've never heard it mentioned so I can't say.'

'You could find out, couldn't you?' Arthur was reluctant to give up. 'You know, wait till he's in a good mood, while you're having coffee together one morning, that sort of thing.'

'I don't know, Arthur. I've hardly been there long enough to start delving into matters like that.'

'I'm sure you could drag it into the conversation. Ask whether he's a shooting man, like your husband. That should do it. Then it'll seem natural for you to enquire whether he shoots over the farm.'

'I see you've got this all worked out,' said Rose, not really put out. 'All right, I'll see what I can do but don't hold your breath. I'm not going to risk upsetting my boss just for your benefit.'

But Rose need not have worried about upsetting Cameron. He was pleased with her work and told her so. He had developed the very habit that Arthur had surmised, often joining her in the office for a morning coffee. Initially business driven, their conversation soon expanded into exchanges of family information, although Rose still hesitated to pursue Arthur's enquiry. And, before she felt able to do so, Cameron made a request of his own.

The property business records had been tidied up thanks to Rose, and she had produced spreadsheets listing tenants, rental income, maintenance costs and other information in an easily comprehensible form. Now Cameron was keen to expand that side of the business but, to make the most of the opportunities, he needed investors. To that end, he informed Rose, he wanted to invite a few people over one evening to discuss the possibilities. To help make the evening flow more smoothly, would Rose be willing to help by acting as hostess?

It was a request that caused Rose some concern. Her inclination was to say yes; she enjoyed her work and was pleased that Cameron had been generous in praise of her efforts. She would like to help promote the business if she could, although the role of hostess would be new and did not come naturally to her. But, for some indefinable reason, she was reluctant to agree. She thought the best way to resolve the issue was to discuss it with Arthur.

A couple of days after Cameron had mooted the idea, she mentioned it to Arthur, including her indecision about whether to attend.

'Seems OK to me, Rose. What's the problem?'

'Oh, I don't know. I don't really see myself as a hostess,

do you? Making smart conversation with Cameron's rich friends seems a bit above my station. I wouldn't want to embarrass him by dropping some social clanger.'

'Don't be ridiculous, woman.' Arthur was quite incensed. 'You're as good as them any day. And you've been to plenty of business dinners with me where you've had to mix with the directors and high-powered customers. You always managed perfectly well then, so why not now?'

Rose still seemed doubtful. 'It doesn't seem quite the same thing. They were social events but this is business. I'm not a professional hostess, just a book-keeper.'

'Yes, but you've done a good enough job for Cameron to have faith in you so I can't see why you don't go ahead. You'll be fine.'

'Perhaps you're right.' Rose tilted her head, still harbouring some nebulous doubt. 'I think it's expected to be quite a late night.'

'I expect so, if the drink is flowing.'

'Would you be all right with that?'

'Why ever not? You've been out late before, for heaven's sake.' He was puzzled by her reluctance. 'You seem to be making difficulties, Rose, which is not like you.'

She frowned while studying a non-existent feature on the wall. 'I just want to be sure I'm doing the right thing, that's all. Not letting anybody down.'

'I'll tell you what,' offered Arthur, wanting to end this vacillation, 'you'll be doing Cameron a favour, right? In return, ask him about the shooting on the farm.' He was only half joking.

'That's all you think about,' said Rose with a thin smile. It was a more accurate assertion than she realised.

˞

Rose followed her inclination and went to Cameron's social-cum-business evening. She applied her make-up with unusual care and dressed smartly in a dark-blue dress that she'd worn to one of Arthur's work's dinners. Arthur even complimented her. 'They'll be bowled over,' he said.

As predicted, it was a late evening. A taxi ferried Rose home at half past one in the morning. Arthur woke sufficiently to ask how it went, was assured it had gone quite well, and promptly went back to sleep.

Rose was tired, but her mind kept replaying the events of the evening and it was well over an hour before she drifted into a restless slumber.

☙

Less than a week after playing her hostess role, Rose had some news for Arthur. She made it as a playful, throw-away announcement, although she could predict his reaction. 'By the way, I've asked about the shooting on the farm. There is no formal arrangement apparently, just verbal permission given to a couple of locals.'

'Brilliant!' Arthur's delight was manifest. 'Well done you for asking.'

There was more. 'I asked if he'd be willing to give you permission as well. He said he would.'

'Even more brilliant. I can hardly believe it.' He laughed before adding, 'I'd begun to wonder if you'd ever ask. But thanks, Rose, it was really good of you.' Arthur paused for a moment, ordering his thoughts. 'I've had something on my mind recently – well, if I'm honest, ever since you got the job. I had a feeling the shooting wasn't tied up and I made some enquiries that seemed to confirm it. But what I've got in mind would be a much bigger step for both of us.'

Having roused Rose's curiosity Arthur now stopped, which made her impatient. 'Out with it then, Arthur, because I've had the feeling you've been dreaming something up for weeks.'

'Right, here we go. You know, of course, that the brothers

sold the business a couple of years ago. Well, it's not been the same since. We've gone from being our own bosses of departments to being part of a group with ever more bosses we hardly know and never-ending demands for this and that. I'm fed up with it, Cliff's fed up and Derek's already gone, as you know.'

He paused again before continuing. 'If I could get a lease on the Manor Farm shooting, I'd give up my job and finish my working life doing something I enjoy. We don't have a mortgage. The brothers looked after me when they sold, so we're not desperate for our next meal. I think we could manage pretty well.'

'For heaven's sake, Arthur, where has all this come from?' Shocked at the magnitude of the proposal, Rose struggled to find a suitable reply. 'This isn't some sort of pipe dream is it? Have you really thought this through? You're not due your pension for quite a while.'

'We'd be all right. If I got the shooting lease, I'd be my own gamekeeper. I've helped run our present shoot all these years, so I know what I'm doing. And I know enough people with money to fill syndicate places. That should cover costs and leave something for us as well. Plus, you'd be working at the farm; that would help.' Arthur was getting into his stride. 'There's another thing, too. There's the former keeper's cottage that seems to be let at the moment; you would know about that. If we could rent it and let this place out, we'd manage even better.'

Rose sat back in her chair, took a deep breath and then slowly exhaled. She did not reply immediately but studied her husband quizzically. 'Well, you could knock me down with a feather. You are a beggar, Arthur, hatching all this up and not saying a word until now. You've knocked me a bit sideways.'

'I didn't want to say anything until I'd worked it all out. I knew you'd find it a big deal, so I wanted to be well prepared. It may be a dream, Rose, but it's not a pipe dream. If everything falls into place, I'm sure we could do it.'

'That's the point, Arthur – if everything falls into place. That's expecting a lot. And where do I fit in to all this? Even if you get the shoot and the cottage – it is let on a short-term tenancy by the way – what makes you think I'd be happy to live in such an isolated spot?'

Arthur was ready for this. 'Yes, it's on its own but I doubt it's a mile from the village, so you could be here in two minutes. You've got your own car and if that broke down you could easily walk it, a fit woman like you.'

'Thanks for that, Arthur. You really have thought of everything.' Rose shook her head in amused disbelief. 'It's really strange; there's me thinking you'd be happy to get permission to pot the odd pigeon or two, and all the time you're plotting some high-flown scheme to turn Manor Farm into something rivalling Sandringham. Are you expecting to invite royalty?'

He grinned ruefully. 'Come on, you're blowing things out of proportion. I know I've set my sights high and it might very well not work out. But it's worth a try, isn't it? If we don't ask, we don't get. At least say you'll think about it.'

Rose did think about it. Over the following week she thought of numerous questions, put them to Arthur and he provided answers. Most of his replies she found reassuring, a few less so. But in response to her query about what he expected her to do all day, Arthur gave a spur-of-the-moment reply that struck home. Rose loved their dogs and was a competent handler; why not develop a sideline in breeding and training gundogs? Pups commanded good prices if they came from proven working stock, and trained dogs even more so.

It was an idea that appealed to Rose. Perhaps it was the

catalyst that finally brought her to a more favourable view of the project. Arthur was right: they had no mortgage, the house was too large and the twins both worked away, Kieran in the RAF and Kerry nursing. Neither would be affected, provided Arthur and Rose retained their house. More importantly, she had been aware for some time that Arthur was no longer enamoured with his job and sympathised with his desire for change. There seemed no compelling reason why they should not pursue the idea, and yet still Rose hesitated.

Her ambivalence centred on a personal dilemma, something of her own making that she refused to address, let alone resolve. It was too difficult. Locked in a quandary, Rose tried to banish it from her thoughts, a problem permanently exiled to avoid resolution. It was not an entirely new dilemma; she had experienced a similar problem twenty years before. But, since she was utterly unable to discuss this difficulty with Arthur, there was eventually little choice but to go along with his plans.

It only remained to decide how best to proceed. Eventually they agreed Rose should suggest a meeting between Arthur and Cameron to sort out the shooting but without mentioning their enhanced plan. That would fall to Arthur when he thought the time was right.

It was soon arranged. They met at Cameron's house one dull, drizzly afternoon, just after lunch. It was not one of Rose's work days, so there would be no distraction on Arthur's part. Within minutes of their re-acquaintance, Arthur was reminded of Cameron's restlessness; the man had a never-ending need for activity, whether lighting another cigarette or fidgeting with a pen. He found it almost impossible to remain still. He seemed anxious to be the perfect host to his older visitor, concerned whether Arthur was comfortable, and if he would like a cup of tea or coffee or something stronger. Arthur was politely accommodating and, suitably reassured, Cameron's excessive attention slowly subsided.

It would be best to talk about farming first, Arthur thought, anticipating that it would put Cameron at his ease. And so it proved, not least because they shared a host of common acquaintances. In fact, this tactic was so successful that time began to get on and Arthur became concerned how he might change the subject. Eventually there was a moment's pause in the conversation and, very politely, he referred to the purpose of his visit.

Cameron was very obliging. He was perfectly happy to give Arthur permission to shoot pigeons over the farm, provided he was aware there were two others with similar permission. Would it be best to cooperate with them? This posed a dilemma for Arthur. It was clear Cameron had no inkling that Arthur might be interested in much more than just pigeon shooting. But if he agreed to work with the others, his pursuit of a sporting lease would surely become more complicated, if not pushed back beyond the horizon.

Arthur decided to go for broke. He thanked Cameron and said he would be happy to cooperate, replaying Cameron's exact words, just as he'd been taught on the best sales courses. They had also taught something else: sell more. 'By the way, Cameron, have you ever considered bringing back game shooting to the farm? There's terrific potential, and a sporting estate commands a very useful additional income.'

It was calculated to arouse interest and it succeeded. Cameron's response was cautious rather than enthusiastic but he was prompted to ask questions. Arthur answered with understated care, realising too much detail at this stage might be fatal. That stimulated another twenty minutes' conversation, during which Arthur casually mentioned that he might be interested if the game shooting were restored. At the conclusion of their talk, Cameron said he would give the idea some thought.

As he drove home, Arthur was pleased with the outcome. It was clear that Cameron was more interested in the prospect of additional income than in participating in the shoot himself. But that suited Arthur; he knew where he stood. If money was Cameron's main motivation then that was the aspect he would play up. Beyond that, it would be mainly a question of cost and whether Arthur could afford it.

Rose was keen to hear how it went, and Arthur was keen that she should hear, although his briefing started oddly.

'He's a strange man in some ways,' he began, 'a bundle of nervous energy. It becomes a bit wearing after a while. After half an hour I felt as though I could do with one of his cigarettes, just to calm my own nerves. Everything is so intense, even asking if you want tea or coffee.'

She laughed in sympathy. 'You should worry; I have to put up with that all the time. But he means well, and I don't notice it so much now. I must have got used to it. Anyway, it's better than having a wet blanket for a boss.'

'If you say so, but I found it quite tiring. I'm not surprised his wife's taking a sabbatical, if that's what it is. She must be worn out, poor woman, coping with that and the children as well.'

'Yes, perhaps,' said Rose doubtfully, before continuing. 'But who knows what goes on in other people's marriages.'

Her dismissive tone suggested she had no wish to pursue the subject, so Arthur went on to relay the course of his talk with Cameron.

'So where do you go from here?' asked Rose at the end of the briefing.

'I said I'd leave it with him for a week or so and then get back in touch to hear what he thinks.' Arthur frowned in concentration. 'It might be helpful if you mention how pleased I was to meet him. In fact, any good word you can put in for me would be useful. As long as you don't give too much away.'

'I've no idea what you mean by that,' responded Rose tetchily. 'You need to remember I go there to work, not to arrange your future lifestyle.'

'All right, keep your hair on.' Taken aback at her response, Arthur tried to mend fences. 'It's just that I thought we were going for this together, that's all.'

'Fine, as long as you understand that it's not down to me to arrange everything. It's your idea and you should follow it through. I'll do what I can, but don't rely on me to talk Cameron into fulfilling your pipe dream.'

Arthur bridled at the words 'pipe dream' but thought better of pursuing it. Instead he let the subject drop, not least because Rose removed herself to the kitchen. He picked up the paper and gave it a cursory look, but his attention was occupied with Rose's recent remarks. In truth, her vehemence had rather shocked him. Such outbursts from Rose were rare and Arthur was at a loss as to the cause. Was she not really in favour of his proposal, only going along with it to please him? Surely not; it seemed to Arthur they had examined every possible facet in exhaustive detail, and to Rose's eventual approval. If not that, then what was the problem?

It was a puzzle, that was for sure, and one for which Arthur had no explanation. But from somewhere deep in his mind he recognised a faint echo, the sound of a chord struck twenty years ago when Rose had suddenly become unhappy.

※

Rose's outburst was not repeated, nor was she noticeably unhappy. If she seemed subdued, even tense at times, it was probably because a major change was being considered and she was in the middle of it. When there was progress in talks between Arthur and Cameron, she was pleased, though hardly ecstatic. Cameron agreed in principle that game shooting could be revived on the estate and that Arthur would have first refusal at reaching acceptable terms. If further progress was slow, it was because it was not Cameron's priority, however much it was Arthur's.

This delay coincided with a request that Rose accompany Cameron to a property development seminar. This would entail travelling to London and an overnight stay in a hotel. Rose conveyed this request to Arthur with manifest doubt. She told Arthur how she had pointed out that her presence was not strictly required; Cameron was the key person and she was merely the hired help. But he was insistent, she explained, claiming that it would help her understanding of the property business and enhance her ability to manage minor decisions in his absence. She could understand the logic but…

Arthur was more sanguine. There was some sense in what Cameron said, he could see that. As for going away with her boss, well, it was all part of running a business. It happened all the time and he was inclined to make a joke of it. Arthur was sufficiently reassuring that Rose eventually agreed to go. However, it was noticeable during this period that the shooting lease was never mentioned, although it was certainly prominent in Arthur's thoughts. Progress had been such that the last thing he wanted was his wife causing any disruption by upsetting her boss. Better by far to go along with Cameron's wishes. After all, it wasn't as if Rose would have to pay.

And so she went. Cameron picked her up from the house and they departed for 'the Smoke', as Arthur was wont to call London. Rose telephoned him at lunchtime the following day with the news that there was to be a question-and-answer session that would run into the evening. Cameron wanted to attend but it would mean their travelling back very late so Cameron had proposed that they stay another night, if Arthur had no objection. She would prefer to come home, even though the hotel was lovely, but Cameron was very keen to stay and Arthur knew what he was like about getting his own way.

Arthur did know, although he was a little perplexed why the Q-and-A session would run so late. There must have been a seminar programme, in which case the organisers were somewhat incompetent in not running to time. The promotional meetings that Arthur had attended finished as scheduled, most attendees being keen to get home. But this was an investment seminar; perhaps they were different. In keeping with his policy of avoiding any possible disruptions where Cameron was concerned, Arthur found it convenient to agree.

~

The news that Caroline Easton and the children were returning to the marital home came a couple of weeks after Rose's attendance at the seminar. It came completely out of the blue to Rose who, since Cameron spoke frequently about his family and saw them regularly, thought she would have picked up some indication.

When she conveyed the news to Arthur, his first reaction was concern about the prospective shooting lease. Would it cause more delay or even end any possibility of an agreement? He had no way of knowing Caroline's involvement or attitude in such matters. He barely knew the woman, their acquaintance limited to the briefest exchange of pleasantries when their paths crossed at the village stores.

Had Arthur not been so preoccupied with his own concerns, he might have noticed Rose's change of temperament sooner. She became vague and irritable, given to long periods of silence. It was an intensification of her recent moods, but it took another invitation for it to become more obvious.

'We've been invited to afternoon tea at the Eastons'.' Rose conveyed this information without detectable enthusiasm. 'Caroline called in today. She's returning this weekend and said she'd like to meet us. She seemed to know about the shooting lease, because she said it would be an opportunity to come to an arrangement.'

Arthur's face lit up. 'She said that? I can't believe it. We must be closer to a deal than I thought. Was Cameron there?'

'No, just Caroline.' Rose was still expressionless. 'She stayed for some time. It seemed to be some sort of "get to know you" visit.'

'Well, you must have got on OK if she's asked us to the house.' Arthur found it difficult to restrain his delight.

'Yes, she seems very pleasant.' Beyond that observation, Rose had nothing to add.

'Right, so what day are we going? It'll have to be a weekend if it's afternoon tea.'

'Sunday, around three o'clock.'

'This Sunday?' Arthur voiced his surprise. 'That seems quick if she's only moving back this weekend.'

'Don't ask me; that's what she said.'

'You don't sound very enthusiastic. Has she said something to put you off?'

'No. As I've said, she was very pleasant.'

Arthur gave a quizzical frown. 'Then what's the problem?'

'I don't suppose there is one,' answered Rose, although her tone suggested otherwise.

'Then why the long face?' Arthur was not entirely lacking in assessing his wife's moods.

'Oh, I don't know. Perhaps it's the thought there will be two of us women in the house. Cameron's forever popping in, asking me to do this and that, not always to do with work. I'm not sure how that will go down with Caroline. I wouldn't be too happy if I were her. It wouldn't be so bad if I was in the farm office – at least that's separate from the house.'

'You're not exactly in the house though, are you? It's an office in a former outbuilding, more a sort of annexe.' Arthur was still perplexed. 'Surely that shouldn't be a problem.'

Rose was not reassured. 'I don't know. All I can say is I wouldn't like it if I were in her shoes. And I'm not sure I want to put the arrangement to the test.'

Arthur heard this with mounting alarm. 'Steady on, Rose. You seem to be anticipating problems even before they've arisen. Surely it's best to see how it goes. You said you got on well with the woman.'

She gave her husband a long, level look from which commitment was absent. 'I'll think about it.'

~

By Saturday morning Rose had thought about it. When breakfast was finished, she announced her decision without preamble. 'I'm going to give in my notice to Cameron.'

For a moment Arthur sat unmoving at the table, shocked into silence. He regained speech only with difficulty. 'You can't mean it.'

But Rose was certain. 'Yes, I do. I've thought about it and that's what I've decided. I just can't see it being a workable arrangement.'

'Wait a minute, Rose.' The import of Rose's announcement had struck Arthur like a physical blow. 'You're talking rubbish. I've no idea what's led you to this but what about me? I'm involved too, remember. I've spent weeks and months working towards a change of lifestyle – one you've gone along with – and now you're almost certainly stymying it without so much as an explanation.

I'm lost for words, I really am.'

Arthur's bafflement quickly turned to something close to anger. If Rose had nothing to say, Arthur was suddenly articulate. 'You've let us come all this way, within reach of a complete change of life, and now you want to throw away that chance. You know how I much I want to leave the firm. I've done thirty years there, for crying out loud.' He made it sound like a prison sentence.

'I know you'd like to get away,' muttered Rose, now more defensive. 'But I'm the one who would have to cope with both Cameron and Caroline. You've no idea how demanding he is. Yes, he's charming with it, but it's pressure just the same. The thought of having to cope with him and Caroline is more than I can bear.'

'For God's sake, woman, you only work there twice a week. That's nothing, is it? Surely you can manage that?'

'It's all right for you, Arthur – you're not so closely involved. You've no real idea what he's like.'

'Hang on a minute, Rose.' Confusion clouded Arthur's face. 'I thought your problem was with Caroline, but now you seem to be saying it's Cameron. Make your mind up. Which is it?'

Rose would not look him in the face. 'Oh I don't know. I'm just fed up with the whole business. I wish I'd never gone there.'

'Well I don't. If you hadn't got the job, we would never have had the chance of a change. We're so close, can't you see that? I know we could still fail to reach an agreement, but there's a world of difference between trying and just giving up. Because that's what your resignation would surely mean; any chance of a deal will go out the window. I can't imagine Cameron taking kindly to you leaving when he's gone to all this effort and expense to bed you into the job.'

For the first time, Rose's expression softened. 'No,

Arthur, I'm sure you're right. It wouldn't go down at all well.' She spoke as if she had inside information.

'Then why not hang in there, at least until we know whether we can reach an agreement? If we can get a signed lease, that's different. Then you can leave whenever you fancy, although it would be best to leave it a while to avoid any ill-feeling.'

Rose managed to look him in the face. 'I know it means a lot to you, Arthur, and that I'm being selfish, which is unforgiveable.' She paused, before adding, 'I'm not always as good a wife as you deserve.'

'You're talking rubbish again, Rose. You do me fine, as you well know. Perhaps I'm asking too much of you, although it hardly seems so to me.' Arthur hesitated for a moment. 'But can't you hang on with the Eastons for a while, for both our sakes?'

Rose studied the mantelpiece as if hoping to find an answer there. Her face betrayed an agitated tautness, which Arthur found unsettling; it was an expression he had rarely encountered before.

It was some seconds before Rose spoke again. 'All right, Arthur. Let's see how it goes on Sunday.' At last she looked him in the eye. 'Let's see how we all get on and then we can make up our minds.'

~

Caroline Easton studied her guests while her husband was speaking. She did so surreptitiously while maintaining the kind of permanent, benign smile one might display for guests not of the first order. Not that she was in any way condescending, for that was not in her character, but her interest in the visitors was far more acute than was required for polite neighbourliness.

The husband, Arthur, was not difficult to assess. She knew him slightly, although this amounted to little more than chance encounters around the village. Now, seated on the sofa, he seemed outwardly relaxed as he allowed Cameron to make the early conversational running. But she detected – or thought she did – a faint hint of anxiety or tension within him. Perhaps it was impatience that was visible in the tiny crow's feet around his grey eyes, an impatience to proceed beyond this introductory small talk and get down to business. After all, that was the main purpose of their meeting.

There was little or nothing she could dislike about Arthur. Intelligent, respectable – she chided herself for using the word – and with a solid background in farming services that Cameron would find very reassuring. A little dull perhaps, hardly a man to set a woman's pulses racing. But who wanted exciting neighbours? No, as a long-term tenant and neighbour, Arthur would be the perfect example.

Rose was far more interesting. She sat next to her husband, stiffly upright, hands folded primly in her lap, patently not relaxed. So obvious was her discomfort that Caroline wondered if they had had a disagreement before coming. And Rose had hardly spoken a word since arriving.

They were not an obvious pairing, that was for sure. There was the noticeable age difference, not huge but sufficient to prompt idle curiosity. And where Arthur was quiet and still, Rose was a picture of suppressed energy. With an insight sharpened by personal experience, Caroline sensed in Rose an earthiness and sensuality entirely lacking in Arthur, a sensuality perhaps constrained by years of practice.

Caroline smiled inwardly. Oh, Rose, what stories could you tell me if we were friends rather than … what? Rivals? No, hardly that. Could they become friends? And if not friends, could they be compatible neighbours? That was what Caroline needed to determine, a decision she must reach within the next hour or so.

※

They had almost reached agreement, Cameron and Arthur. Leaving their wives to their own devices, they had withdrawn to the kitchen to hammer out a Heads of Agreement, and they were nearly there. Arthur and Rose would occupy the old keeper's cottage and restore it at their own expense. Because of its run-down condition, a costed list of improvements would be drawn up and agreed, obviating the need to pay rent.

The shooting rights were more easily settled. The woods and spinneys, long neglected, would be managed by Arthur who, to Cameron's surprise, submitted a written programme of improvements including coppicing and planting. Game-rearing equipment would be bought and installed at Arthur's expense. Cameron would make some farmland available for game-cover crop and be recompensed by Arthur. None of this proved difficult to agree.

The sticking point was the duration of the sporting tenancy. After half an hour's intense discussion they were still far apart, and the impasse seemed to herald the end of the discussions. They rejoined their wives.

'Well,' ventured Caroline, 'have you reached an agreement?'

'Not far off,' said Cameron quietly, although his face expressed disappointment.

'And may I ask what the problem is?' Caroline was not inclined to let matters rest solely with the men.

'We've agreed pretty much everything bar the term of the tenancy.' Cameron sounded a shade irritable as he continued. 'Arthur wants fifteen years but, really, that's out of the question. I've never heard of such a long term before.

I've offered seven but that's as far as I can go.'

Caroline turned to Arthur. 'May I ask why you think fifteen years is necessary?'

'It's the investment, Caroline. It will cost thousands to upgrade the cottage…'

'But it will be rent free for a period,' interrupted Cameron.

'But mainly it's the work of improving the woods.' Arthur was on surer ground here. 'All the woods are very neglected, overgrown, too thick, too thin, no understorey in most of them. It will take me between five and seven years to get them under control and better suited for pheasants. A seven-year agreement won't allow me to start seeing a return for all that work.'

'I see.' Caroline sat back in her chair, contemplating the two positions. She did not contemplate for long. She stood up, took Cameron's arm and addressed both Arthur and Rose. 'Would you excuse us for a moment?'

'Yes, of course,' replied Arthur. 'In fact, I'd welcome a breath of fresh air. Would you mind if we had a walk round the garden?'

'Not at all; help yourselves.' Caroline the hostess was making her presence felt. 'When you're ready, there'll be another cup of tea waiting for you.'

※

At first Arthur and Rose barely spoke as they sauntered along the edge of a flower bed, although neither paid it much attention. They turned behind a rather dilapidated garden shed, which hid them from the farmhouse. Here Arthur stopped, but it was Rose who spoke. 'It's a nice place they've got here.' A safe comment, if vacuous.

'It would be better if wasn't hemmed in by all these barns and workshops. But it's a working farm, I suppose, so business has priority over the view.' Arthur pulled a wry face and changed the subject. 'I wonder what Caroline is saying to him.'

'Yes, that was odd, wasn't it? The way she took over.'

'She seems quite a determined sort of character.' Arthur pondered for a moment. 'It's easy to forget her family owned the greater share of land when the farms were merged. I've no idea what the legalities are, but it's possible her share is held in trust or something similar. Just because she married Cameron doesn't mean the farm becomes his. Rather the opposite, if I know anything about farmers. They're very precious about their land.'

Rose was distracted by another thought. 'There's no sign of the children. They don't seem to be here, which is odd if she's moving back in. I would have thought the whole point was to get the family back together under one roof.'

'Maybe. It's not really our business though, is it?' Arthur looked at his watch. 'How long should we stay out here, do you think?'

'Are you going to hold out for fifteen years?' It was the first interest Rose had shown in the negotiations, and her tone was neutral even now.

'It's what I'd like, Rose. We'd be making a huge commitment and fifteen years would take me up to pensionable age. By that time, well, we'd have more options. We'd see how we felt.' He sucked his teeth and squinted at nothing in particular. 'I'd settle for twelve years, I suppose, but ten would be pushing it. I wouldn't feel comfortable with that.'

They made their way back to the house

Caroline was as good as her word: a fresh pot of tea was available for those who would like another cup. Only she took the opportunity, the other three apparently more interested in the outcome of their various discussions.

Rose and Arthur resumed their places on the sofa, sitting side by side but both now more upright and tense than before. Cameron sat in his armchair, seemingly relaxed although his face was deadpan. Only Caroline seemed unaffected by the atmosphere, busy with her cup of tea and remarks about her plans for the garden. These prompted little response. After a minute or so she stopped speaking and looked at her husband expectantly.

It was Cameron's cue. 'Caroline and I have considered your proposal for a fifteen-year term and, in view of the remedial work you propose to carry out, we are happy to comply.'

That was all. He offered no congratulations or expressions of pleasure, nor did he shake hands. He merely gave a smile, somewhat forced, like that of a man confronted by two awkward choices who opts for the lesser evil. But even Arthur found it difficult to express his delight, overcome by the realisation of a long-anticipated dream that had become something of an obsession.

~

After the Dennisons had left and Cameron had taken himself off on some work-related chore, Caroline was able to reflect on the afternoon's events. She was satisfied with the outcome and her role in reaching agreement. Not that she was particularly intent on restoring game shooting to the farm, although the social side certainly appealed to her. No, her unspoken interest lay in Rose Dennison, the part-time employee of Cameron's burgeoning property business.

And Caroline had found it a fascinating exercise getting to know the reticent Rose. That she was not normally so reticent was a certainty; Caroline's few, discreet enquiries had soon established that. And someone so shy and tongue-tied was hardly likely to have been considered by Cameron as a suitable hostess, a role of which Caroline had learnt only some time after the event, just as she had learnt of the seminar trip.

So when the men had retired to the kitchen to conclude their discussions, it had given Caroline an unmissable opportunity. Instinctively she liked Rose; despite her reticence she appeared wonderfully down to earth and practical. More importantly, Rose seemed guileless, her character far removed from that of a natural conspirator. And it had been Rose who raised the subject of her office within the house and her reservations about its suitability. Bless you, Rose, for your diplomatic consideration. Caroline did not disclose that one of a number of conditions for her return to the marital home was the removal of the office from the house. And it had been a close-run thing whether Rose would have to go, too.

Although two meetings could hardly be considered sufficient for her to say she knew Rose well, Caroline was satisfied. She had seen enough to believe she could live in proximity with Rose, and with Rose's soon-to-be-more-distant proximity to Cameron. That was a great relief. She was sure they were not rivals, but whether they were unequal partners sharing a single resource was another matter. In the circumstances, she felt able to settle for that.

❧

Arthur's visit to the town began badly and then got worse. His appointment with the solicitor had fallen through because the wretched man called in sick. The letting agent barely detained him for twenty minutes instead of an anticipated hour, and now his friend Graham had called off their lunch date.

Never mind, thought Arthur, as he drove back. There was always something to do on the shoot now that he was working for himself. And the nature of gamekeeping is such that work is never finished, merely temporarily completed until its resumption the next day. But what some might regard as a disadvantage, Arthur relished and happily embraced.

He left his car at the barn and put the time to good use by topping up some feeders and inspecting his earlier coppicing, which was opening up the wood nicely. This had brought him within a ten-minute walk of home, where a cup of tea would be most welcome.

He followed the track as it wound its way through the wood, the trees now clothed in a delicate green tracery of unfurling leaves, for the sap was rising strongly in the early April air. And it was through this hazy green filigree that Arthur first glimpsed the house. At the edge of the track, his black Labrador picked up the scent of some passing creature, quite recently if her keen interest was any guide. Normally Arthur would have noticed this immediately, but his attention was caught by something else.

To one side of the house was a lean-to woodstore and, beyond that, a long timber shed. A vehicle was parked in the space between, largely screened from view. Arthur stopped. For several moments he stood and stared, too absorbed to register a woodpecker's strident drumming somewhere in the distance. It was a sophisticated 4x4, metallic grey, just like Cameron's.

Arthur stood motionless but he was thinking the more. Perhaps a query about business or pleasure. Not that he would say anything, or even hint at it. Don't rock the boat; those were Arthur's watch words. Nothing could possibly be gained by any other course of action, rather the contrary. He remembered a tutorial he had attended in his previous working life, the proposition that most contracts contain a hidden cost. This sporting lease was no different and perhaps Arthur had understood that, even as he put his signature to the paper.

He turned and spoke to the dog. 'Come on, Jess. Let's go and find another job.'

The Taste of a Stranger

HÉLÈNE DE BRESSON stood just inside the doorway, watching and waiting. Her prospective tenant stood by the window staring into the middle distance, while his young wife lingered near the fireplace, also waiting. But Bernard Vermeulen was not a man to be hurried. Although only a few years older than his wife, he possessed a gravitas that would normally be expected of a more mature businessman. When he finally spoke, it was as if he were addressing the window. 'The apartment may be suitable…' He paused, his heavy brow furrowed in concentration. 'But the rent you are asking seems a little high.'

Hélène had expected nothing less. However, she was an astute people watcher and had observed that the wife was very much taken with the apartment. She also guessed the couple had not been long married, and that the husband would be loath to disappoint his new bride. In short, she was certain she had the measure of her man. 'I think Monsieur will find the rent quite reasonable for such a spacious apartment in this town. And so convenient for your business needs, if I have understood your requirements correctly.'

A pregnant silence fell between them. At last Bernard Vermeulen turned his gaze from the window and addressed Hélène directly. 'Very well, Madame, we will take the apartment.'

Hélène permitted a small, gracious smile to flicker across her aquiline features. It was a small enough victory over Bernard Vermeulen, but it pleased her.

※

With their business completed and the Vermeulens gone, Hélène returned to her own apartment within the house. Her husband glanced up from reading the paper. 'So, are we to have the pleasure of such charming new tenants?' Gustave de Bresson, self-styled writer and poet, tended towards florid language, as if compensating for his literary failures.

'Yes, Gustave, I have obtained a new tenant.' Her husband did not react to Hélène's emphasis on the first-person singular. But then he was not businesslike and had long ago abdicated any responsibility for their financial affairs in favour of his wife.

'If I heard their accents correctly, I don't believe either is French.'

'He is Belgian, from somewhere near Liege. He has a business – selling hats, would you believe – that requires a great deal of travel around Europe. I suppose that explains the ridiculous car. The back is absolutely full of boxes.'

Gustave smiled. 'I think it's American. A station wagon, I believe they're called. Hardly suitable for many of our roads but magnificent all the same, if you are hoping to impress your customers.' Perplexity overtook curiosity. 'So what, may I ask, brings them to our humble town? I haven't noticed that Lorraine is particularly short of hats.'

'It's hardly our affair,' responded Hélène, more interested in having secured a new tenant. 'But he mentioned that business in Germany is more difficult now, since the occupation of Czechoslovakia, although I'm not sure why unless he's Jewish. That might explain it.' She had no time for politics, inhabited as they were by absurd, posturing men. 'He said he felt somewhat vulnerable living near the German border, whatever that means. Personally, I don't care what brings them here as long as they pay the rent.'

Gustave sighed with quiet exasperation. Unlike his wife, he was only too well attuned to current affairs, which he considered at great length but without ever achieving any certain – let alone consistent – opinions. He changed tack. 'The wife is very pretty. Is she Belgian too?'

'No, she's English, I believe. She didn't say much but her French is good, picked up in Paris by the sound of it. She seems a little in awe of her husband, although he took the apartment to please her.'

'They're a very cosmopolitan couple: Belgian and English with an American car, but who've decided to move to France.' Gustave chuckled. 'Yes, very cosmopolitan. I'm already looking forward to their company.' He fell into silent contemplation, perhaps imagining the pleasures of the kind of rich, cultured conversations so conspicuously absent in his relations with Hélène. 'Yes, indeed,' he continued, as though speaking to himself, 'they are a very handsome couple.'

He suddenly turned to his wife and addressed her directly. 'Perhaps we should revive our challenge.'

This proposal was not entirely unexpected by Hélène, who reacted sharply. 'No, Gustave, I won't do it.' A look of bafflement suffused her face. 'Surely it's time you gave up these games. You're a middle-aged man, nearly fifty – and, besides, you always lose.'

Gustave was sensitive about his age but his shaving mirror still allowed his vanity a certain reassurance. 'As you well know, I was only recently forty-eight – and I don't always lose. There was the Austrian woman, if you care to remember. And I also remember that you were not in the least averse to such challenges in the past.'

'Perhaps, but we were both younger then. As for the Austrian woman, she must have been blind as well as stupid.' Hélène frowned. 'Now it just seems pointless, as well as risking a good tenancy.'

'Pah!' Gustave's disappointment lent unusual force to his words. 'Is that it? A fabricated excuse, if ever I heard one. My God, how dull you've become, Hélène. Your avarice has taken over your life. Every last spark of vitality seems to have been crushed under the weight of your obsession with money. Yes, you still dress well and are meticulous with your appearance, but that show is like a husk. There is nothing underneath.'

Hélène only just managed to contain her temper. 'My ability to manage money is the only reason you live so well today. Left to you and your family, we'd have been bankrupt and homeless years ago. So you listen to me, my fine dilettante friend: you continue to while away your days with your cronies at the Station Hotel, playing cards and solving all the world's problems, and leave me to see that there's food on the table and a roof over your head when you return.'

Gustave knew when enough was enough. 'Yes, yes, yes. Everyone knows you are a woman of exceptional abilities.' He might have added, 'But a dull shadow of your former self,' but he thought better of it.

☙

A week later the Vermeulens moved into the apartment. A bright May day gave a more pleasing aspect to the plain, stuccoed façade of the house, which was large but insufficiently grand to warrant being described as a château. Hélène had utilised an excess of living space to provide additional income. An elderly couple, the Cartelets, occupied the former stableman's accommodation at the rear of the house. The semi-invalid husband tended the substantial cottage garden, while Madame Cartelet often cooked for the de Bressons. In view of these services, Hélène charged a reduced rent.

At the opposite end of the house, Hélène had overseen the conversion of surplus rooms into a separate apartment, although it was accessed through a shared front door. This was to be the Vermeulen's apartment. It being already furnished, the Vermeulens brought only some decorative items to make it more homely.

Hélène welcomed them from the doorstep and instructed her maid, Amelie, to help unload the station wagon. Hélène gave most of her attention to Elizabeth Vermeulen, advising her on the better shops, market days and similarly useful domestic information. Then she withdrew but continued to observe from the shadows of an upper window as the Vermeulens fetched and carried their possessions.

She had to acknowledge that Gustave was right; they were a fine-looking couple, the husband solidly built with a saturnine, intelligent face that was more Latin than Teutonic. His wife was a classical English rose, even to the strawberry-blonde hair that was now somewhat tousled from exertion. Hélène watched her struggle to extract a large box from the car and admired the suppleness of her body.

Perhaps Gustave's words had struck deeper than she – or Gustave – had thought. On reflection, maybe she had become a little staid, her interests now reduced to a limited span of domestic and financial management. Not much given to introspection, Hélène's unusual bout of self-scrutiny drew the equally unwanted conclusion that Gustave's description of her as 'dull' might well be more accurate than she cared to admit. But Hélène was also capable of assessing her merits. At forty years of age she remained a handsome woman, still blessed with a good figure even if it was thickening slightly around the waist. She had never been pretty, her strong features attractive in the way that a lioness is distinguished from a gazelle, but a lack of conventional prettiness had proved no handicap in attracting men. A sharp intelligence and instinctive guile had made Hélène more than a match for most men, a compelling but formidable challenge to any would-be suitor.

When the Vermeulens had finished unloading, the husband drove the car to the former stable yard at the side of the house, parked it and returned to his new apartment. Hélène continued to stand at the window, as if in a reverie. After a minute or so, she smiled an uncharacteristically broad smile as if some inspired idea or revelation had suddenly emerged from the fog of her own thoughts.

Later that day, just before retiring to her own bedroom, Hélène turned to Gustave. 'By the way, I've been thinking about your recent admonition. Perhaps I was a little dismissive. Therefore I've decided to accept your challenge.'

Then she was gone, leaving Gustave open mouthed with surprise, but none the less pleased for that.

The Vermeulens soon settled into their adopted home. Bernard Vermeulen resumed his commercial travels and was frequently away for two or three days, sometimes more. When they were first married, Elizabeth had often accompanied her husband but, although sometimes interesting, the incessant travelling and a succession of undistinguished hotels had soon palled. Although occasionally tempted to accompany him on short tours of the more scenic parts of Europe, Elizabeth now preferred to remain at the apartment.

Time did not hang heavily for such a lively mind. A classical – if unfinished – education had imbued in her a love of prose, poetry and art. In some quiet, secret moments, Elizabeth was inspired to put pen to paper herself, although she was modest about her abilities. Indeed, finding time for just such opportunities played no small part in her welcoming the move to Lorraine; she was a woman quite at ease in her own company.

Not that Elizabeth was left to her own devices for long. Perhaps it was just neighbourliness on Hélène's part, the invitations to accompany her when she visited the shops or the market, or it could have been simply to ensure Elizabeth had company in the strangeness of her new surroundings. Whatever the reason, Elizabeth was appreciative of the attention and, within a week or two, they were friends. Through Hélène, she began to learn the quirks and pretensions of the town's more prominent citizens as well as those at the opposite end of the social spectrum. Elizabeth noted the respect the market traders and shopkeepers accorded Hélène, an unspoken acknowledgment of her swift but rigorous shopping habits; no one was less likely to be short-changed or passed off with second-rate produce.

Hélène greeted or acknowledged many people during these walks and engaged a number of them in conversation, although she did not always introduce Elizabeth. After one particularly frigid acknowledgement to an obviously well-to-do woman – it was reciprocated in kind – Elizabeth was sufficiently curious to query the cause.

'She doesn't like me,' was Hélène's blunt explanation. In a rare moment of self-revelation she continued, 'There are many in this town that dislike me. When Gustave first brought me here after the war, it soon became clear that a certain section of society thought he had married beneath him. I had no aristocratic lineage or money from trade; even worse I came from Alsace and spoke with that mistrusted accent. Alsace may be French again but, with their Germanic links, many Alsatians do not welcome the change and these people know it.'

To Elizabeth's surprise, Hélène was not yet finished. 'We were not completely ostracised or ignored. When I was with Gustave most people would speak pleasantly enough, but if I was alone then I suddenly became invisible. I noted their hypocrisy and, as our circumstances have improved over the years, I now enjoy their evident discomfort.'

This was the first of several observations by which Hélène conveyed her view of the town's inhabitants and her relations with them. Elizabeth took such confidences as a sign of their growing friendship. Indeed, she felt increasingly able, perhaps even obliged, to reveal more of herself. But in view of Hélène's greater maturity and obvious abilities, it was only natural that Elizabeth tended to defer to her companion. It was not quite a friendship of equals; their age difference – almost a generation – and, more pertinently, their very different lives, lent a subtle bias which favoured the older woman.

Elizabeth's relationship with Gustave was very different. On learning of her interest in literature, Gustave could scarcely contain his delight. His bookshelves – or library, as he called it – were immediately thrown open to her, along with his personal opinions on an extensive range of writers such as Baudelaire, Rousseau and Voltaire. He did manage to curb an urge to expound on the various French literary movements, suspecting that existentialism or nouveau roman might have only limited appeal to a spirited young woman. But it was when he discovered Elizabeth aspired to write that Gustave believed he had struck gold.

He presented Elizabeth with a collection of his own poems, a slim volume published soon after the war when he was living in Paris. Inspired by the recent conflict, much of his writing addressed struggle and sacrifice. That single volume represented the high point of his literary career, although other pieces had occasionally been accepted by some of the more obscure literary magazines.

Whatever Gustave's limitations as a writer, Elizabeth found him to be a charming and erudite companion. Tall and elegant, he possessed a pleasing demeanour that both men and women found attractive. His fine features were made distinguished by flecks of grey hair at his temples and a flamboyant, soldierly moustache. It was an appearance that conformed to Elizabeth's idea of a literary mentor although, naturally, this thought remained unspoken.

Elizabeth was soon a frequent visitor to Gustave's library. They made a lively couple, their conversations often punctuated by laughter for Gustave possessed a wry wit more appreciated by Elizabeth than Hélène. So when Gustave suggested he and Elizabeth select a subject or storyline and then assess each other's writing, it was with a sense of both anticipation and some apprehension that she accepted. Gustave was delighted. Indeed, since Elizabeth Vermeulen's arrival, there was altogether a new spring in his step, a renewed zest for life that did not go unnoticed by his wife.

ॐ

It was an odd circumstance of the de Bresson household that there were few visitors. Gustave's social life centred on his friends at the Station Hotel. This was a clique comprising men of some means who were able to escape from business or domestic ties with fair regularity. Gustave's great friend was Hunblot who, among numerous other interests, owned a small factory in the town that produced aluminium kitchenware. Many years earlier, Gustave had been persuaded – without consulting Hélène – to invest in this enterprise and his reward included a seat on the board of directors. Although this investment provided Gustave with a veneer of respectable business interest, profits proved thin and had permanently damned his financial competence in Hélène's eyes.

While Gustave was frequently absent from the house, few visitors other than tradesmen ventured to the door. Hélène seemed content to conduct her social life in chance encounters around the town. But Elizabeth became aware of one exception; this caller came irregularly, usually in the evening and always using the side door rather than the front. Elizabeth also noticed Gustave was rarely in the house during these visits, and that Hélène conducted her business with this visitor – for such seemed to be the purpose – in the small, ground-floor room which served as her office.

Elizabeth's curiosity was aroused, not least because her glimpses of the man were fleeting but indelible. Although of average height, he evinced an extraordinary physical strength. This manifested itself in a broad chest and powerful, sinewy arms. His legs were commensurately sturdy, giving his gait what Elizabeth at first thought might be a sailor's roll until she suddenly realised it was a limp. On the rare occasions their paths crossed there would be the merest inclination of his head in acknowledgement, but Elizabeth was struck by his glance, a brief glimpse into liquid brown eyes of unfathomable depths.

When Elizabeth felt sufficiently confident, her natural curiosity impelled her to ask about this visitor. Hélène smiled at the enquiry, as if it were not unexpected. His name was Manien, she explained; he was a well-known figure about the town, but about whom there were conflicting stories. Principal among these was that Manien had served in the latter stages of the war and been severely wounded, hence the slight limp. Apparently the limp was not Manien's only injury. It was strongly rumoured there was another wound, a livid scar in the shape of a cross scored directly above his heart. The more credulous, said Hélène, believed Manien's life had been saved only by divine intervention, although she forbore to add that it was mainly women who seemed susceptible to this version.

Nor did Hélène disclose an alternative rumour, which carried more credence among the men, that Manien had past connections with Marseilles and even colonial Algiers. These stories attributed his injuries to nothing less than wounds incurred during involvement with the notorious Marseilles' dockland underworld. Manien's taciturnity and solitary nature did little to dispel either narrative.

Hélène was more forthcoming about Manien's living. He was an insurance agent, an employment in which he appeared to succeed in spite of his natural reticence. He was, Hélène declared, a cleverer man than some allowed and very well informed. She did not, however, divulge the exact nature of their business, leaving Elizabeth with the impression that Hélène merely helped with his paperwork.

In fact, their association went back nearly a decade. A damp, gloomy October evening had not deterred Gustave from attending the Station Hotel, leaving Hélène alone in the house. On answering a knock at the side door, she had found Manien standing in the near dark. Hélène knew him only by sight and by rumour.

'Good evening, Madame. I have a business proposition for you.' He spoke very quietly, but with perfect assurance.

After a moment's hesitation, Hélène responded in kind. 'Then I should like to hear it.'

A small smile had accompanied Manien's brief nod of satisfaction, his judgment vindicated. In the course of his work, he explained, he had learned that a prominent citizen was in financial difficulty due to gambling debts. To help pay off these debts, he needed to sell a tenanted cottage. The man wanted this done quickly and with complete confidentiality. The price reflected these requirements.

There had been a brief pause, then Manien began to answer Hélène's unspoken questions. Manien was greatly impressed by Madame's hard work in restoring the de Bresson's fortunes. He was sure she would recognise an advantageous deal, as well as possessing the necessary discretion. He finished by naming the rental income and the purchase price.

Hélène could indeed see the advantages, but she was also shrewd enough to ask why Manien did not buy the cottage himself, or how he might benefit otherwise? Manien's reply had been forthright; he did not have sufficient money himself, but the vendor would reward him for finding a suitable buyer. He wanted nothing from Madame, with just one minor proviso: he would like to co-operate with her if further opportunities arose in the future. It was a proposal that bound Hélène more securely than a signed contract.

If only Manien had known of the marginal improvements to the de Bresson finances at that time, he might have thought twice before knocking on Hélène's door. But it was true she had restored their finances from troubling debt to something approaching credit-worthiness. The former stableman's cottage had been made fit to let, and one end of the house – it was not large enough to be called a wing – had been converted into the apartment now occupied by the Vermeulens. Hélène alone had instigated and overseen these changes, although they had scarcely made the de Bresson's rich or even noticeably well off.

But Hélène had well understood the singular nature of Manien's proposal and set about obtaining the necessary funds with vigorous and telling persuasion. With Gustave an ill-informed and passive bystander, Hélène played ruthlessly on their improved finances and the de Bresson name until a reluctant bank relented and advanced a loan. She acquired the balance in cash from a close acquaintance who ran a successful service business in Metz. Thus the cottage had been acquired, the first of Hélène's co-operative ventures with Manien.

Elizabeth's curiosity elicited only such minimal information as Hélène thought fit to reveal. Hélène had long ago learnt to regard information as a precious commodity, to be gathered, filed and stored until such time as its value might best be realised. Only time and Hélène's discretion would allow Elizabeth to learn more.

❧

Within a month of moving into the apartment, the Vermeulens had settled into something of a routine. Bernard Vermeulen continued his business travels, usually returning to his wife at weekends or for a midweek overnight stay if his route allowed. These journeys continued to include major cities in Germany, where his customers assured Bernard that all was well. They were sure that, with the future of Eastern Europe's ethnic Germans now settled, the creation of a Greater Germany would see business opportunities increase; some even urged Bernard to exploit the opportunity.

But as the spring of 1939 gave way to summer, Bernard Vermeulen became a subtly changed man. He found it increasingly difficult to view the prospects of his family's business with any degree of optimism. His attention to international politics became increasingly burdensome as his natural seriousness drifted steadily into pessimism. He viewed the new German–Italian political agreement – the Pact of Steel – with dismay. Major sporting events or new film releases now induced in him nothing more than a feeling of irritability, an impatience that the world could continue to concern itself with such trivia. The opinions of others regarding the international situation received increasingly short shrift, a tendency that the more perceptive members of his family and friends noted with some concern.

Elizabeth might have been equally concerned about her husband's worries had she been less distracted by the de Bressons, but the novelty of a new home and the insistent attentions of her landlords left little time for introspection. Inspired by Gustave's infectious enthusiasm for French literature, she read a great deal, not least delving into the complex love life of Flaubert's *Madame Bovary*. An appreciative and eager reader, these books prompted Elizabeth into vigorous discussions with Gustave about the motives and behaviour of the characters. Being young and full of life herself, it was hardly surprising that Elizabeth sympathised with the frustrations of Emma Bovary, trapped in a dull marriage to a weak man. Like Hélène, Elizabeth found politics incomprehensible, boring and faintly disquieting. She found it far preferable to immerse herself in the chequered lives of vivid fictitious characters inhabiting an often turbulent world, but where she was completely safe.

Hélène provided additional distractions by taking Elizabeth on her regular trips to Metz and, for occasional variety, Rheims. Travelling by train, these visits were ostensibly for shopping and indeed included some window shopping for the latest women's fashions. But in Metz Hélène's priority was always to see a particular friend. Cecile Laurent had loaned the balance of money towards Hélène's first property purchase. Somewhat older than Hélène, well preserved and formidable, she ran a thriving business with iron discipline. Her principal interests were a bar and café situated a little distance from the prime shopping area, although this did not seem to affect trade adversely.

On their first visit Elizabeth was introduced to Cecile, but it became clear she would not be included in whatever was to be discussed between the two friends. Instead she was passed – courteously, but with little option to refuse – into the care of a good-looking young man whom Cecile plucked from the bar expressly to show Elizabeth the city of Metz.

Elizabeth might have been discomfited by this arbitrary action had not Xavier proved to be a pleasant and knowledgeable companion. Of similar age to Bernard, he said he was a former army officer, although his career seemed to have been surprisingly short. It was also unclear why he should be found so often in Cecile's bar when not obviously employed there. But, since he claimed to have been stationed in the city's garrison, he was well placed to escort Elizabeth around the tourists' Metz. And Xavier lived up to his word, first visiting the cathedral of Saint Stephen, where he proved able to laud its Gothic architecture as well as expound on the city's ancient Gallo-Roman history.

It was a procedure that soon became a pattern. Hélène went to Metz every fortnight, always inviting Elizabeth until it became such a regular practice that her presence was assumed. Another pattern was also established. After a coffee and some polite conversation with Cecile and Hélène, it would be suggested that Elizabeth would be far better engaged viewing the sights of Metz. Xavier would be procured from the bar and off they were expected to go. On the one occasion that Xavier was not available, Cecile seemed to have no difficulty in securing another good-looking young man as a substitute.

Elizabeth was not naïve; she quickly became aware the bar was a meeting place for couples, some of whom preferred to use a discreet side door. She also had her suspicions about the availability of private rooms upstairs. But, brought up in Paris as the daughter of a British diplomat, her explorations of the more exciting areas of that city had broadened her education. Whatever Elizabeth's concerns about the nature of Madame Laurent's business, or being temporarily passed into the care of a young man, they quickly dwindled to nothing. She enjoyed the walks around the city, and the congenial nature of her escort added to the pleasure.

Since moving into the apartment, Elizabeth had sometimes wished for a friend more similar in age. She had tried befriending Hélène's maid, Amelie, but she remained no more than politely cordial. Much as Elizabeth admired Hélène and valued her friendship, she was sometimes faintly resentful of her dominance, so reminiscent of her own mother's. Now these visits to Metz, with their mix of shopping, tourism and interludes of younger companionship, albeit male, soon came to exert a considerable attraction.

It was on one of their return journeys that Hélène first broached the subject of Elizabeth's companion in Metz. 'Do you find Xavier acceptable company while Cecile and I are busy?'

Since this was not the first time Elizabeth had been placed in his care, she was a little surprised at the question. 'Yes, quite acceptable, thank you, Hélène. He is very knowledgeable about the city's history, and the walks along the rivers and islands are really lovely. Today he showed me the opera house.'

Hélène considered for a moment. 'Good. And he behaves himself, I trust?'

'Yes, perfectly.' She smiled at Hélène's concern. 'He is very much the gentleman.'

'Even better, then he will not incur Cecile's ire. But I can't believe he doesn't flirt with you. What red-blooded man could resist such an opportunity?'

This was a subject on which Elizabeth felt rather defensive. 'Well, I'm not saying it hasn't occurred, but it's lightly said and easily ignored.'

Hélène's response was unexpected. 'My dear Elizabeth, I know you are English but you really must learn the French habit of flirtation. It will add immeasurably to your enjoyment of life. You have the undivided attention of a handsome young man and you do nothing? Surely not.' She leaned forward and placed her hand on Elizabeth's arm. 'Flirtation is an art beyond the value of jewels. Done well, it reduces men to malleable clay.' She closed her hand to emphasise the point.

Elizabeth smiled uncertainly and, in the absence of a reply, Hélène continued. 'What do you tell your husband about our little visits to Metz?'

'Oh, I tell him about the different sights and historic buildings I've seen, and what an interesting city it is.' For some unaccountable reason, she felt obliged to continue. 'Bernard has been there on business but he said we'll have to go as tourists one day and I can show him round.'

'And do you mention that you are accompanied?'

Elizabeth answered with defensive care. 'I haven't mentioned Xavier by name, no. Actually, when I say something like, "we went to the opera house", I'm afraid I probably give the impression I went with you. I hope you don't mind.'

Hélène gave a rare laugh. 'My dear girl, you've said exactly the right thing. Flirting is one thing but it's best not to make it too obvious to one's spouse – unless provoked, of course.'

They both laughed and Elizabeth was surprised to feel a little relieved. Perhaps the situation with Xavier had concerned her more than she had realised. The absence of any homily or judgment from Hélène was reassuring, perhaps implying a degree of complicity. After all, Hélène had instigated these accompanied tourist excursions, so she was hardly in a position to criticise Elizabeth for going and enjoying them. And it was all perfectly innocent, even if she omitted to tell Bernard every last detail.

But Hélène had not yet finished. 'Has my husband made a pass at you yet?'

Elizabeth's shock was palpable. 'Oh Hélène, how can you say such a thing? Gustave is the most perfect gentleman, and so knowledgeable. I've learnt so much and he's given up no end of his time…' Her defence petered out into silence.

'Come now, there's no need to upset yourself.' Hélène offered a conciliatory smile. 'It's just that I know Gustave too well. He never could resist a pretty face and yours is prettier than most. And you share his love of books, all discussed and dissected at leisure in his private library. My God, what more could he ask?'

'Do you want me to stop going there?' Elizabeth's concerns were crowding in. 'Should I avoid seeing Gustave?'

'Certainly not! It would break his heart, just when he has found a new lease of life.' Hélène leaned forward and took her hand. 'But it's best that you know, then you won't be surprised when it happens. All I ask is that you treat Gustave kindly. He's like a boy in many ways, with his enthusiasms and weaknesses. He's never quite grown up.'

'But don't you mind?' Elizabeth was still uncertain. 'I mean, knowing your husband looks at other women.'

'My dear, I rather think Gustave has gone much further than just looking. But we are adults in this life, Elizabeth. We all have to come to terms with our spouses' weaknesses. I discovered Gustave's many years ago; it wasn't the end of the world.' Hélène's words became more confiding. 'In fact, our spouses' weaknesses can provide a certain licence, you understand, for activities such as an innocent stroll around Metz.' Head tilted and eyebrows raised, her eyes conveyed something more than just amusement.

Elizabeth was still unsettled. 'Are you sure you don't mind Gustave and I meeting in the library? God, it sounds worse as I say it.'

'Nonsense!' Hélène was enjoying this role. 'He so enjoys your little discussions that it would be cruel to stop them. No, just be kind, humour him and everything will be fine. Besides, I need you to keep him out of my hair – and out of the Station Hotel.'

This observation dispelled any doubts. 'Well, if you think it's all right, Hélène. I'm not sure I could be so generous, or forgiving.'

'We have to be sensible about such matters. You should do the same.' She added slyly, 'After all, how can you be sure your husband hasn't a doting female or two secreted away somewhere on his travels?'

'I hardly think so.' Elizabeth gave a wry smile. 'Bernard's too preoccupied with other things at the moment.'

Seeing Elizabeth was not inclined to say more, Hélène allowed their conversation to lapse. But, as she appeared to turn her attention to the passing countryside, she was considering their conversation. What had she achieved? Foremost, at one stroke, she had almost certainly damned Gustave to the permanent role of literary mentor rather than that of the Lothario he so earnestly desired to be. That thought amused and pleased her in equal measure. And yet she had managed to ensure Gustave would continue to have his muse frequently in his company, fated to look upon her beauty but never to touch. Hélène savoured that prospect with unalloyed pleasure.

Her thoughts turned to Elizabeth. Within a few weeks of their first acquaintance, Hélène had realised her companion was not the naïve, starry-eyed newly-wed of first impressions. Elizabeth's acquiescence in the matter of Xavier, and her instinct to omit this detail from her husband, indicated a welcome degree of independence.

This knowledge provided Hélène with two more pieces of the jigsaw she so loved to construct. Added to the pieces already in place, Hélène's slowly emerging picture was of an Elizabeth who might still have much to learn about life, but who also possessed something of a free spirit that was, perhaps, waiting to be liberated.

❧

With time on her hands, Elizabeth enjoyed the luxury of choosing her activities. As spring became summer, she took the opportunity to borrow a bicycle that languished in the de Bressons' old stable. Cleaned, oiled and tyres newly pumped up, she took to exploring those areas beyond walking distance of the apartment. These roads took her outside the town into the countryside. The only drawback was the hills, which sometimes called for more strenuous pedalling than she cared for. Not infrequently she was reduced to dismounting and pushing the cycle uphill.

One route avoided overmuch hill climbing. It was a road that followed the river valley and it provided manageable inclines as well as all the beauties of the countryside. The landscape was varied: fields of hay and corn, interspersed with woodland on steeper outcrops of uncultivated land. The river, a tributary of the Meuse, made its placid way between banks lined with alder and willow, some hung with clusters of mistletoe.

This route became a favourite of Elizabeth's but it was on one of these excursions that a minor disaster occurred: a puncture in the rear tyre. The bicycle had a repair kit in the saddlebag, but she had only repaired a puncture once before and that was in the front wheel. Removing the rear wheel, with its attachment to the chain, was a different matter.

She studied the problem for several minutes, growing more frustrated as time went by and no solution presented itself. Being only a couple of kilometres from town, she resigned herself to walking home.

As Elizabeth lifted the cycle to begin the long walk, she was surprised to see a man approaching. He came from the nearby riverbank, from the direction of a stand of willows, although she had not previously noticed him.

'Bonjour, Madame.' He spoke softly, a pleasantly modulated voice with a faint but unfamiliar accent. 'Are you in difficulty?'

'Yes, I'm afraid I have a puncture. I have a repair outfit but I'm not sure…'

'Ah, then permit me to be of assistance. I see the problem is with the rear wheel. We must find out exactly where.'

With no further ado, he picked up the cycle as though it were a feather and strode off towards the river's edge. Elizabeth followed, noting that his stride, although firm, was affected by a slight limp. It confirmed what she already knew: her unexpected saviour was Hélène's shadowy colleague, Manien. Following behind, her feelings were a mix of gratitude and curiosity tinged with the faintest hint of apprehension.

Manien proved a swift but silent puncture mender. In very little time the tyre was levered off the wheel rim, the inner tube partially withdrawn and the puncture located by immersing the tube in the river. During this procedure Elizabeth took the opportunity to study her helper. As she had already observed, he exuded a powerful sense of physical strength. This was echoed somehow in his face which, although modestly attractive, was not outstandingly handsome. On the few occasions he looked at Elizabeth, she was immediately aware of his dark-brown, liquid eyes. They possessed a strange, mesmeric quality, in which she imagined it would be quite easy to drown.

The puncture was soon repaired. Manien pushed the cycle back to the road and Elizabeth followed. 'There you are, Madame; that will get you home or allow you to continue on your way, if that is what you wish.'

'Thank you.' Elizabeth was effusive in her gratitude. 'Thank you so much. You've saved me a long walk. Will you take something for your trouble?' She began to open her purse.

He held up a hand in refusal. 'No, Madame. It was nothing and I want nothing.'

Nonplussed, Elizabeth was unsure what to say. 'Well, I hope I haven't interrupted your work.'

'Not work, Madame; I am merely fishing. My punt is tied up in the willows.'

'I see.' She was aware of his scrutiny. 'I must let you get back to your fishing then. Thank you again, I really am most grateful.'

Reluctant to leave without making some sort of gesture, she held out her hand. Manien shook it briefly, his own hand enveloping Elizabeth's. She mounted the bicycle, smiled in his direction and started to pedal away.

'Au revoir, Madame Vermeulen; perhaps we'll meet again.'

Elizabeth was too surprised to reply.

❧

With the warmer summer days, it became Hélène and Elizabeth's habit to take lunch in a corner of the walled garden, sheltered from the strengthening sun by the shade of a fine cherry tree. Beneath its generous canopy, the two women passed their time in desultory conversation while enjoying a glass of wine.

Hélène's newfound confidences extended to revelations about herself. Once having broached the subject of men with Elizabeth, it was as though Hélène had overcome an invisible barrier in their relationship. This new sense of confidentiality now displaced any previous inhibitions.

During their walks around the town, Hélène would point out a fellow shopper and confide that the woman was, or had been, involved in an extra-marital affair. This happened on several occasions and yet, despite her avowed dislike of the town's bourgeoisie, she never condemned the alleged perpetrator. In fact, Hélène was notably forgiving, always offering mitigating circumstances such as a neglectful or adulterous husband. She conveyed a sense that a woman was perfectly entitled to seek comfort elsewhere if her marriage proved unsatisfactory. It was nothing more than the French way.

It may have been the garden's languorous atmosphere or the wine that loosened Hélène's tongue, although she was a hardened drinker. In the sultry heat, the conversation often meandered around to accounts of Hélène's earlier life when she had lived in Paris immediately after the war. It was there that she had met the aspiring writer, Gustave, and been swept up both by him and the bohemian culture of the Left Bank. Hélène's stories often concerned the free and easy lifestyles of their Parisian friends and she took pleasure in recounting their numerous affairs and jealousies. At first, she kept a discreet veil over the more lurid details of these affairs but, as time passed, the veil became ever more diaphanous and Hélène's descriptions became a veritable tour of love's many permutations.

Elizabeth found these anecdotes greatly entertaining. The generous glasses of wine contributed to her enjoyment, perhaps adding humour or pathos beyond what the tales would otherwise have borne. As Hélène delved ever more deeply into her colourful store of memories, the combination of heat, alcohol and the measured modulations of Hélène's voice sometimes induced in Elizabeth a feeling of extreme lassitude, which she struggled to overcome. On other occasions it made her libidinous.

Hélène also enjoyed these post-lunch conversations.

Her instinctive reserve steadily melted away, assisted by an equally instinctive desire to prise any secrets from the heart of her companion. But in her many tales of literary jealousies and sexual carousels, Hélène carefully avoided saying anything too explicit about her own behaviour. She freely acknowledged having been tempted but had a gift for leaving Elizabeth uncertain whether she had actually succumbed.

Hélène was a mistress of this kind of verbal sleight of hand and used it frequently. It was during one such ambiguous anecdote that Elizabeth's curiosity was suddenly overtaken by impatience. 'I wish you'd say whether you actually went with this man, rather than leave me hanging in suspense.'

Hélène was sure the wine was speaking, but was not at all put out. 'My dear Elizabeth, I long ago learnt the value of discretion; it's a force of habit with me now. But I'll make an exception in your case – on one condition. I will tell all, if you will do the same. We'll be like two schoolgirls swapping indiscretions behind the bicycle shed.'

Elizabeth giggled at the idea. 'But I don't have anything to tell. My life has been extremely dull compared to yours.'

'Oh, I'm sure that's not true. For example, were you a virgin when you married?'

Elizabeth was a little taken aback but heard herself answer. 'I knew a boy when I lived in Paris, the same as you. He was very nice, a student like me. We were young and unattached, so we got together on a few occasions.'

'Just a few? You disappoint me Elizabeth. And does your husband know?'

Elizabeth frowned in concentration. 'D'you know, Bernard has never asked. He knows I went out with other boys, of course, but that was before we met. It's two different eras, if you know what I mean: before Bernard, and after.'

Hélène smiled an acknowledgement. 'And anyone else? You mentioned boys in the plural.'

'No, they were just occasional dates. I told you, my life has been incredibly dull by your standards.' Elizabeth sipped her wine but, remembering, suddenly looked up. 'Oh, I had a crush on one of the senior girls at school.'

'Really? How interesting. And was it reciprocated?'

A flicker of doubt crossed Elizabeth's mind but she felt too committed to stop now. 'Well, it was never full on or anything, but she invited me to her to her room a couple of times. She was a prefect, with all its privileges. I was supposed to be practising my French oral – but probably not in the way the teachers envisaged. Mostly we just talked, had an occasional cigarette and, well, you know…' Elizabeth gave a wry laugh. 'I'm not sure I should have told you that.'

'Elizabeth, when I was in Paris Sapphic love was practically de rigueur. And I should know. More to the point, did you enjoy it?'

Elizabeth considered for a moment. 'It was all right. Yes, I suppose I must have done, otherwise I wouldn't have gone back to her room again. Anyway, she moved on to university soon after that, so it didn't last long.'

'And have you mentioned this little episode to your husband?'

'No, I haven't! What a thing to ask, Hélène!'

'Not at all. Many men find the prospect quite stimulating, particularly if it concerns their wives. And there is a school of thought that says a woman's sexuality is not complete until she has experienced lovemaking with another woman.' Hélène studied Elizabeth with amusement. 'Possessing that initial qualification, perhaps you should consider studying for your degree.'

Elizabeth professed puzzlement. 'Whatever do you mean?'

'It's really quite simple. The average man is just that, average in bed. They are the indifferent, the mediocre, the perfunctory, the selfish and the drunken. That is the average man after a year or two of married life, dulled by over-familiarity with his wife and the drudgery of domesticity. He begins to stray in search of more excitement, but that doesn't make him a great lover.' Hélène was now in full flow. 'But, hidden among the average, there are those who understand that lovemaking is an art only learnt through diligent application. They make an infinite study of a woman's needs and desires and commit themselves totally to fulfilling them. Such people – and they can be men or women – are rare but, once experienced, well…' Her expression was more explicit than any words.

'I see,' was all Elizabeth could manage in response.

In the absence of any further comment, Hélène continued, 'Gustave likes to think he is in that super-man category, but I can tell you he isn't. I won't embarrass you by asking about your husband.'

Elizabeth smiled her relief. 'No, I think that would definitely be a step too far.' But the tone and delivery of her response was not lost on Hélène.

Hélène had taken a dislike to Bernard, put off by his intensity and perpetual air of gloom. She thought they were a less well-matched couple than they first appeared, the more so as she got to know Elizabeth better. But she was scrupulous in hiding her dislike, making a special effort to appear sympathetic. She took the opportunity to do so now.

'How is your husband, by the way?' Hélène never referred to him by name. 'The poor man seems to carry the weight of the world on his shoulders.'

'He's fine, although he worries about the future of the business.' Elizabeth frowned. 'He's concerned there will be a war and goes on about it until both of us are equally upset. But what can I do about it, Hélène? I thought it was all supposed to have been settled last year at Munich, but Bernard says that was just a temporary reprieve. I don't understand; why would anyone want to start another war after the disaster of the last one?'

Unusually, Hélène had little to offer. 'I'm sure I don't know. Gustave also gets quite worked up about such things but that's nothing unusual. One day he's fearful of the Germans and the next he's fulminating against the communists and socialists, who are apparently a worse threat to France than the Germans. I gave up listening long ago. I've no time for politics; it's run entirely by men, don't forget, and therefore capable of any folly.' She picked up her wine glass and gave Elizabeth a sardonic smile. 'We should mind our own business and enjoy ourselves while we can.'

꙳

Later, back in her apartment, Elizabeth looked back on this conversation. With the passing of alcohol-induced bonhomie, she viewed their discussion in a different light. Rather than any concern about the nature of her revelations to Hélène – although these provoked a minor qualm or two – it was Hélène's stark categorisation of men and husbands that unsettled her. For, when she considered Hélène's frank discourse on the nature of men's sex drive, it brought what had been a vague disquiet into much sharper focus. Judged by Hélène's categories, there was little doubt in which one Bernard would be placed. Although loath to admit it, for Elizabeth the physical side of their marriage was proving something of a disappointment.

It had started well enough after the wedding and continued so for the first few months. But she now realised that Bernard's mood had changed after the recent German occupation of Czechoslovakia. Was it possible that such events could intrude even into the bedroom? It had been concerning enough that this event had persuaded Bernard to move from Liege, and yet he hadn't recovered his good humour since taking the apartment. If anything, he had become increasingly depressed.

Elizabeth felt very much out of her depth. When comparing her experience of men with Hélène's, she realised how little she knew. At least there was one crumb of comfort, although it was meagre enough. If Hélène's theory was correct – and it sounded worryingly plausible – there was a reasonable chance that Elizabeth herself was not the source of the problem, something she had begun to question. On reflection, Xavier had left her in no doubt of his interest, as had Gustave, although more obliquely, as Hélène had confirmed. At least that offered some reassurance. But as to Bernard, Elizabeth had not the slightest idea what to do or even whether anything could be done to improve their relations.

❧

It was unusual, and unfortunate, that Gustave returned home early from the Station Hotel one July evening for, on entering the house, the first thing he heard was the indistinct sound of voices, one female and the other male. The voices came from Hélène's office where, as Gustave immediately realised, she was closeted with Manien. This put him in an even worse mood than that brought about by an argument at the hotel, where strongly differing opinions about the international situation had deteriorated into harsh words between the optimists and the pessimists. Vacillating as usual, Gustave had chosen to make a tactical withdrawal.

A little before ten o'clock, Gustave heard the sound of Manien's departure and his wife returning to the living room. He wasted no time. 'I see you've had a visitor while

I was out.'

'Surely you didn't come home early in the belief you'd catch me out, Gustave?' Hélène sounded perfectly reasonable but she knew the signs and prepared for an argument. 'You know I conduct some business with Manien, so it shouldn't be a surprise if you find him here.'

'You make my point for me, Hélène. The fact that you have any dealings with that man is bad enough, but to conduct them in this house is completely unacceptable.'

'I think you're exaggerating, Gustave. I know you don't like the man but, really, it's absurd to carry on the way you do. Our meetings are completely open and above board as you would know, if you were ever here to see them.'

'You've no idea, have you?' Gustave's voice became querulous. 'You've no idea of the comments I have to endure from my so-called friends. Everyone knows Manien's reputation, his dreadful reputation with women, and everyone knows he comes to this house when I'm not here. No wonder I'm the butt of some crass humour. And that's to my face; God knows what they say behind my back.'

'Well, you've just mentioned the solution to your problem. Be here more often, take an interest and make the effort to get to know the man. He's not as bad as you choose to think.'

'There's no smoke without fire, Hélène.'

'Falling back on a cliché, Gustave, and you a man of letters? Surely you can do better than that. And you're wasting your breath if you expect me to change my arrangements.'

'But his background is dubious, to say the least, and quite possibly criminal.' Gustave paused in his search for words, for he was not good at argument. 'It's humiliating to have my wife even remotely linked to the man.'

'There are perfectly good reasons for believing he was

injured in the war. Thousands were, if you remember. Why do you choose to believe the worst?'

'Because nobody can tell you the name of his regiment or even the corps he's supposed to have served in, nor where he was allegedly wounded.' Gustave suddenly remembered another oddity. 'And another thing: how is he able to spend so much time fishing when everybody else is working for a living? Is he such a successful insurance agent that he only needs to work part time? All this makes me – and my friends – deeply suspicious.'

'What would you know about a day's work? This sounds more like jealousy to me. I know him as a straightforward insurance agent who often has to work evenings because that's when people are at home. So what if he sometimes goes fishing during the day? No, these foul stories are just rumours peddled by malicious gossips. They have nothing better to do than speculate about Manien calling at homes to collect the insurance premiums, which is all part of his business.' Hélène chose to play her ace. 'You may choose to be embarrassed by our association, but if you are concerned about any threat to my "honour" then think back on our conduct over the last twenty years and ask what "honour" of mine remains to be compromised, and why.'

Seeing Gustave momentarily silenced, Hélène chose to try and end the argument, for she was not always unkind to him. 'Why don't we change the subject? How are your literary sessions going with the lovely Elizabeth? I hear you've persuaded her to start writing.'

'Yes, she has put pen to paper.' He seemed reluctant to elaborate. 'A couple of short stories and a few poems.'

'And are they any good?'

'There's some promise, but she has a lot to learn.'

'Well, you're just the man to teach her.'

'Yes.' Gustave gave his wife a penetrating look. 'She doesn't come to the library as often as she used to. I wondered whether you'd said anything to put her off.'

'On the contrary, Gustave. She asked whether I had any concerns about your library meetings – Elizabeth can be wonderfully proper – and I assured her that I thoroughly approved. You could ask her yourself, if you doubt me.'

'No, I couldn't do that.' He hesitated. 'It could be that she's spending the time writing, although seeing the hours you two spend lounging in the garden, I am somewhat sceptical.'

'That time is well spent on what you would call research, Gustave. Elizabeth is still young and comparatively inexperienced about life. She is endlessly curious about many things, hence our discussions. You must have found the same thing.'

'Yes, I can't deny that.'

'Well, there you are. And I'm sure you do your best to broaden her mind.'

'What do you mean by that?'

'Nothing in particular, Gustave, although I do know you've introduced her to Madame Bovary and Belle de Jour, among others. Have you got round to de Sade yet, or anything from your special section, the books where the authors prefer to use an assumed name? They would broaden anybody's mind.'

'You can never speak without injecting a little poison, can you, Hélène?'

'I don't mean anything by it.' She smiled archly, in the ascendancy once again. 'But you have to admit, your library meetings, the book critiques, your masterly writing guidance, these are a great opportunity for you.'

'Opportunity?' Gustave sounded dubious. 'What opportunity?'

'Oh, come now, don't play the innocent with me.' She smiled, playing the coquette. 'Our challenge, Gustave; our challenge.'

꙳

Elizabeth left her apartment in search of Hélène, although she would have had difficulty explaining why. Affected by a strange sense of restlessness, she sought friendly company in the hope of being cheered up, or at least diverted. For the first time since moving to the apartment she felt vaguely dissatisfied with life, but was unsure of the cause.

Crossing the hall, Elizabeth passed the telephone and idly wondered why it rang so rarely for the de Bressons. It was, she mused, just another oddity of the de Bresson household.

In this distracted frame of mind, she spotted Hélène's outline through the translucent glass panel of the office door, a room that Elizabeth had never previously entered. Normally she would have withdrawn unannounced, for Hélène could be brusque if disturbed from her routine, but something made her tap gently on the glass. After a moment's delay, she heard Hélène's call, 'Enter,' and opened the door.

The office was small, converted from a former cloakroom. The single ceiling light was just adequate, hardly penetrating into the shadowy corners and giving a dingy air to the dull paintwork. A metal filing cabinet took up a disproportionate amount of space in one corner. Hélène sat behind an old mahogany desk, its green-leather top largely obscured beneath scattered paperwork. The only other item of furniture was a solitary kitchen chair standing in front of the desk, which Elizabeth was now invited to occupy.

'Welcome to my den of iniquity.' Hélène did not seem to mind the interruption.

'Am I stopping you working? I can come back later if you're busy.'

'No, it's no trouble.' She glanced down at the desk top. 'I've almost finished. I'll just clear away this paperwork. Most of it is Manien's; he's not very organised when it comes to documents and policies. I act as his book-keeper. It just needs a tidy mind, that's all. It really isn't hard work.'

As she spoke, Hélène placed papers into different files. Without looking up, she continued. 'You may have gathered that Gustave doesn't approve of my arrangement with Manien, but then he doesn't understand it. He doesn't realise how we – and I include Gustave – have benefited from it over the years. He is concerned only that Manien is the subject of some malicious rumours and that I am tainted by association, and therefore Gustave himself is tainted too.'

This rare personal insight was prompted by Hélène's recent exchange with Gustave; lingering irritation made her unusually forthcoming. 'I don't tell Gustave, but Manien also lodges money here in my strongbox. Neither of us trust the local banks. The clerks know everyone's business, as do the managers. It's no surprise that confidential information somehow percolates through to all and sundry in a town this small, from the mayor to his oh-so-respectable cronies.' Hélène stopped short of adding where she did bank, although it was not difficult for Elizabeth to guess that Metz was the likely location.

These revelations, particularly the association with Manien, aroused Elizabeth's curiosity. 'Manien seems rather controversial. Don't you mind being the target of such gossip?'

'No, it's a small price to pay.' Hélène gave an enigmatic smile. 'Besides, I'm not completely averse to being labelled a scarlet woman. I find it delightfully ironic. Secretly, half the women in this town would die for Manien's attention. The outwardly respectable, the well to do, the religious – yes, particularly the repressed religious – they all harbour their own secret desires. Whereas I, the woman who knows him best, choose not to mix business with pleasure. That is what they find impossible to believe.'

Elizabeth was used to hearing Hélène's trenchant views on human nature but the subject of her association with Manien prompted something more than passing interest. 'Do you think the rumours about Manien are true?'

'He exerts a certain fascination. I'm not completely immune to it myself, so why shouldn't others be susceptible? And once a man acquires such a reputation, that hint of danger seems to add to the attraction, however reprehensible.' Hélène tilted her head in amused contemplation and studied Elizabeth across the desk. 'But then I believe you have now met Manien.'

'Yes, he mended a puncture for me, along by the river. And I've seen him outside the house a couple of times on his way to see you, but he hardly notices me.'

Hélène gave an involuntary laugh. 'My dear Elizabeth, you could not be more wrong. Be assured, Manien has taken note.'

'Hélène, you're pulling my leg. He has barely acknowledged me, let alone spoken, even when he mended my puncture.'

'That is just Manien's way. Don't be misled; he is well aware who you are. Let's just say I've had to field certain enquiries brought about, I'm sure, by something more than idle curiosity.'

Elizabeth sat back in her chair. 'You're just trying to embarrass me.'

'I don't think I've succeeded, although you look so charming when you blush; an innocent abroad in a wicked world.' Hélène gave a knowing smile and continued with her mischief. 'You should be flattered at another man's interest or, at the very least, take it as a compliment. A woman needs to let her husband know there is still competition for her attention, just to keep him up to the mark. And it feeds our curiosity for the taste of a stranger, that secret desire hiding within every woman, however much she may regard it as a perversion or curse.'

Elizabeth laughed. 'You say some outrageous things, Hélène. I'm not sure I ought to listen to you too closely.'

Hélène sensed Elizabeth was surprised to learn of Manien's interest. Perhaps she was curious, or even intrigued. In their recent, more intimate, conversations Elizabeth sometimes let fall occasional delicate ambiguities that were more obscure than Hélène's. Perhaps they were unintentional but Hélène marked them well. 'There is nothing outrageous about Manien, I can assure you. Interesting, definitely, even fascinating – but don't take my word for it. You could find out for yourself if you let me arrange a suitably discreet meeting.'

'I don't think so, Hélène, fascinating as you make that sound. I have no wish to find myself caught up in some awful rumour mill.'

'Oh, you disappoint me, Elizabeth. Passing up such an opportunity seems almost sacrilegious. And you seem to be blossoming as you adopt our French habits.'

'Well, I think it's a pleasure that will have to wait.' Elizabeth meant it to sound flippant but failed. 'I have enough problems as it is.'

Sensing an opening, Hélène chose her words with care. 'Surely you can't mean man problems, Elizabeth? I can't believe that.' A quizzical half-smile played around her lips as she placed her hands together on the desk.

'Oh, it's nothing really. I'm probably exaggerating as usual.'

'I have noticed you've been a little quieter than usual, but…' She left a void for Elizabeth to fill.

'It's just that Bernard worries so, about the business and everything.'

'Of course he does. It's perfectly understandable, with him travelling around half of Europe and all the present difficulties. And he's away so often. It must be a relief to get back here, a return to normality even if it's just for a day or two. Surely that's good for both of you.'

'Yes, of course,' said Elizabeth, although she sounded less than certain. 'It's just that I wish he could forget all his worries when he is here.'

'You haven't been arguing, have you?'

'No, but that's because I won't argue. I walk away when it starts to become too much.'

'We all do that at times, Elizabeth. That's normal married life.'

Elizabeth nodded in apparent acceptance. 'Yes, I understand that; even my parents have occasional crossed words, so I know it's not that unusual. But in our case it seems to have begun quite early; we've only been married a year. I suppose I expected it to last longer before we became like an old married couple. It's a bit disappointing that it's started so soon.'

Hélène declined to offer any solace. 'Early married life can rather shatter illusions. You soon become aware of characteristics in a man that were not evident before marriage. But we learn to cope.'

'Yes, but it's not exactly a thrilling prospect, is it?' Elizabeth glanced across to Hélène. 'There's something else, as well. Bernard has mentioned that it's possible we may move on before long. I probably shouldn't be telling you that, but it seems right to give you some sort of warning.'

Hélène stifled her annoyance at this news, even managing to sound philosophical in reply. 'Well, your husband never made it sound like a long-term arrangement so I can't say that I'm surprised. Is it likely to be soon?'

'No, I don't think so. Nothing is settled yet, so probably not before Christmas.' Elizabeth was suddenly reluctant to reveal more. To change the subject, she followed up an earlier observation. 'Is Manien a photographer as well?

Only I noticed there are some photographs among the papers.'

Hélène hesitated before replying. 'Not professionally, no. But sometimes it's necessary to make a photographic record of an insured item if it's particularly valuable.'

'I see. Yes, that makes sense.' It did make sense to Elizabeth but she was still puzzled. Although the few photographs were small and she viewed them only briefly from an odd angle, her impression – of one photo in particular – was of a room featuring not an object but a person.

Before Elizabeth could consider this apparent discrepancy, Hélène continued. 'Actually, I'm the photographer in this household now, albeit by mischance. Gustave took up photography some time ago but, like so many of his enthusiasms, it soon died. Typically, he bought all the apparatus for developing and printing as well as a good camera, and he had the ideal dark room in the cellar. I helped occasionally and didn't like to see everything lying idle when he lost interest. So I took over, although I've lost interest myself now, except for developing Manien's prints. You can see how Manien and I are interdependent. His work puts him in possession of confidential information, which I help him manage, to the benefit of us both. I ignore the rumours because he is very useful man.' Hélène gave a mischievous smile. 'You really must meet him.'

❧

Back in her apartment, Elizabeth sat reading. Or rather she gave the appearance of reading, for the pages remained unturned as her mind strayed elsewhere. She was contemplating her earlier conversation. Hélène's phrase, 'goųt de l'étranger', the taste of a stranger, had registered with Elizabeth as a distinctly odd expression. Out of curiosity, she considered its meaning. It was hardly something new, this cryptic side of Hélène's, since Elizabeth found many of her utterances distinctly Delphic. Perhaps it was part of Hélène's charm, this ability to impart an air of mystery to discussions about the mundane. But then 'goût de l'étranger' was hardly a mundane topic, if she had understood it correctly. And certainly not when applied to the shadowy Manien.

※

The open space in front of the station was exceptionally crowded. The August holidays had begun but this milling crowd did not comprise holidaymakers. It was made up of soldiers alighting from a train and now being cajoled into some sort of order by their NCOs. A small group of officers watched from close by but did not intervene. Despite the peremptory urgings of the NCOs, several minutes elapsed before the men had arranged their equipment to their satisfaction and fallen in to marching order.

From his position outside the Station Hotel, Gustave was well placed to observe this process. Although it was twenty years since he had been obliged to wear uniform – family connections had ensured he had served largely out of harm's way in the artillery – Gustave knew enough to detect a resigned weariness among the assembled men. Nor was their appearance impressive, with some uniforms not matching or ill-fitting, or both. Here and there men went bareheaded among their helmeted comrades, while a few smoked openly in the ranks. Occasionally an anonymous, acid comment could be heard directed towards the NCOs.

Gustave edged his way through the thin crowd of onlookers. A tall, gangling officer stood a little apart from his fellows, adjusting his troublesome kit. Gustave took the opportunity to address him. 'Are you heading for the fortifications?'

'No,' said the officer, heedless of any need for secrecy. 'We're going to guard the border with Belgium, near

Montmédy, beyond the end of the Maginot Line. In case the Belgians decide to invade France, you understand.' He pulled a wry face at his feeble joke and then, as if aware of the troops' poor showing, felt obliged to add, 'We're a reservist regiment, hence the long faces. They'd much rather be going on holiday, or earning good money at the Renault works.' The officer's pale eyes met Gustave's. 'And we've got to march from here.'

'I see.' Gustave turned his gaze to the soldiers, at last assembled into some sort of military order. 'That's bad luck; you'll be on your feet for quite some time. If you don't know the Argonne region, it's beautiful but hilly.'

'I won't ask how far; morale is bad enough as it is. Let's hope it doesn't rain.' The officer was not a young man, but at least he conveyed a resigned determination to see the march through, even if others should fall by the wayside. 'Ah, we're off at last.' With this comment directed more at himself than Gustave, the officer shouldered his kit and walked away.

They moved off to the sound of studded boots on cobblestone and the faint clink of metal as rifles rubbed against buckles. A loud voice ordered them to get in step but the men ignored it. Gustave watched them go; their long Lebel rifles jutting into the air above helmeted heads but projecting little sense of military power. Rather the opposite: the awkward length of the obsolescent rifles gave a faint air of antiquity, like muskets from a bygone age.

Twenty years before, on the fourteenth of July 1919, Gustave had watched the great victory parade in Paris. Vast crowds had thronged the Champs-Élysées to see the military might of France and pay homage to the sacrifice and prowess of that magnificent army. From a balcony above the crowds, he had seen the remarkable spectacle of the parade which filled the entire length of the Avenue de la Grande-Armée. He had been moved and proud that day.

Now, as the last of the soldiers disappeared from view, he was deeply troubled. He would speak to Hunblot about it.

~

Hélène stood by her bedroom window. Although it was midnight, residual heat from the sun still radiated from the stuccoed brickwork, giving a sultry air. The warmth drifted into the bedroom in barely perceptible zephyrs, gently caressing her face, but Hélène barely noticed, concentrated as she was on the recently expired evening.

She and Elizabeth had spent the time in Elizabeth's living room. Gustave had been out for the evening, as was his habit. Bernard Vermeulen was absent on his commercial travels. Hélène knew he was due to return in two days' time because Elizabeth had told her so.

Although not invited, Hélène had knocked on Elizabeth's door bearing a bottle of kirsch, the colourless cherry-based liqueur for which she knew Elizabeth had a particular liking. She felt in need of friendly company, Hélène explained, an hour or so of frivolous gossip to dispel the gloom. Gustave had returned to the house that afternoon concerned about the state of some soldiers he had seen and was now worried whether the rest of the army was in a similar state.

Elizabeth knew a fellow sufferer when she saw one, and the kirsch was a welcome bonus. The evening had been spent in idle chatter, although Hélène's chatter was rarely idle. As time went on, she again turned the conversation to her life in Paris during and after the war. To Elizabeth's delight, and no doubt heightened by several glasses of kirsch, Hélène finally admitted to having had an affair. And not just one, it soon became clear, but a number. In place of all the previous hints and suggestions of bohemian decadence that had so irritated Elizabeth, Hélène now provided increasingly intimate details of a series of amorous adventures.

But what about Gustave, Elizabeth had enquired. Hélène had a ready answer: Gustave had led the way and, being her own woman, she had simply followed his example. Their relationship had been tempestuous at times but never dull. Unlike now, she managed to imply. Regret did not feature; she was young then, with an insatiable curiosity about people and life. You are old soon enough, she had warned Elizabeth; time is shorter than you think.

It was nearly eleven o'clock before their evening drew to a close. When Elizabeth saw Hélène to the door, she was a little unsteady on her feet, which made her giggle. Although not incapable, Elizabeth realised she was more drunk than usual. Thanks to Hélène's ministrations, she had enjoyed easily the greater share of the kirsch.

Hélène still stood by the window, enjoying the darkness. She was aware of a sense of anticipation that reminded her of her younger self. Leaving the window, she padded silently to the door connecting her bedroom to Gustave's. Listening carefully, head tilted in concentration, she could hear the regular snorts of her sleeping husband's breathing. She had locked the door while Gustave was out earlier in the evening to ensure an uninterrupted night. Satisfied, she walked slowly to her bedroom door which she opened, walked through and then closed quietly behind her.

A small electric torch assisted Hélène's progress to the stairs. Descending to the hall, she passed the telephone on its small table, and the front door, now locked and secured. The windows either side of the door admitted a ghostly light, rendering the torch temporarily redundant.

Hélène stopped in front of another door. Producing a key from within the folds of her nightgown, she offered it to the lock with infinite care, just as she had tested it earlier. The key turned the mechanism with very little sound, although the door creaked audibly as she pushed it open. She needed the torch to locate a new set of stairs, which she ascended as silently as the carpeted treads allowed.

There were three rooms on the first floor but Hélène well knew which door she sought. Once there, she stopped, turned off the torch and listened, but could hear nothing. Placing both hands on the door handle, she turned it gently but firmly. The catch made some sound but the door opened quietly enough. She waited in the doorway until her eyes became accustomed to the meagre light from the curtained window.

The faint sound of breathing came from the large double bed just discernible in the gloom. With small, silent steps, Hélène approached the bed until she was beside it. She could see Elizabeth lying on her back, only half under the single sheet. There was something uncomfortable about her position, as though the heat or the kirsch was troublesome. Her nightdress had been abandoned in the humid warmth and Hélène could see where the sun had left its imprint. That which was untouched seemed to glow in the darkness.

'Elizabeth.' Hélène leaned over the bed and repeated softly, 'Elizabeth, are you unwell? Only I heard you cry out.' The recumbent figure stirred and half-turned her head. 'You gave the most awful cry, Elizabeth. I heard it from the hall. Have you had a nightmare?'

'What? Is that you, Hélène?' Elizabeth's speech was thick, fighting through a fog of sleep and alcohol.

'Yes, it's me. I was afraid you were ill or having a nightmare. But I'm with you now, so everything's fine.' Hélène was whispering as she undid the sash of her nightgown. 'I'll keep you company for a while, just to make sure you're all right.'

The black silk gown shone faintly as it slipped from her shoulders and fell to the floor. Hélène slid under the sheet. 'There now, my darling, you'll be fine now. Go back to sleep.'

꙳

Elizabeth awoke much later than usual, a little before nine o'clock. The sun streamed through the gaps in the curtains, illuminating the bedroom with sharply defined strips of light on one wall and the ceiling. Avoiding looking towards the window – the brightness hurt her eyes – she propped herself up on one elbow. She did not feel well.

Gradually her senses restored to something near functional. She had a terrible hangover, that was for sure. There was no doubt about the cause of the hangover, for they had emptied an entire bottle of kirsch. No wonder she felt groggy. Her glass had hardly ever been empty during the whole evening. Kirsch and women's talk; that's how they'd spent the evening. But she was aware of something else, something nagging away in the fogged recesses of her brain.

Nothing was clear, that was the trouble. There were only impressions, one of which she recalled with increasing clarity. Sometime during the night, she had experienced deep, sexual ecstasy. And Hélène was involved, which made it extraordinary and deeply unsettling. Had she dreamt it? After all, she had recently experienced some disturbing dreams, unknown since before her marriage. And, if truth be told, it wasn't just night dreams; her daydreams also strayed into strange, unsought imaginings, as inexplicable as they were shameful. Shameful, she understood only too well, because they did not involve Bernard. But, confined to a secret compartment in her mind, Elizabeth found the dreams deeply erotic, stimulating an occasional return to adolescent habits.

Sufficiently recovered to be certain something had happened during the night, questions flooded Elizabeth's brain. Not just the how or why but the implications. Since events seemed to centre on Hélène, it was she who became the focus of attention. But that provided no comfort. Elizabeth realised she could barely contemplate the prospect of seeing her, and yet seeing Hélène was a certainty. What on earth was she to say?

Later in the morning, looking out into the garden from her apartment, Elizabeth saw Hélène sitting under the cherry tree, eating her lunch. It was a meal Elizabeth chose to miss, having barely managed a couple of slices of toast for breakfast. Now she faced the dilemma of whether to join Hélène or stay hidden away. But strength of character had never been a weakness with her so, with considerable qualms, she left the apartment and made her way into the garden.

Hélène's greeting was absolutely normal, as was her quiet smile. Elizabeth declined the offer of a glass of wine as she sat down. 'Aren't you eating either?' Hélène enquired and received a shake of the head in reply.

Not knowing what to say, and rather hoping Hélène would initiate any conversation, Elizabeth stared blankly at the table in silence.

'Aren't you feeling very well?' Hélène's tone was solicitous but perhaps tinged with amusement.

'I'm all right, but I have felt better.'

'Yes, I'm sure.' Hélène's smile broadened. 'You did rather hit the bottle last night. Well, we both did. But I don't suppose the damage is permanent. Are you sure you won't have a glass of wine, a hair of the dog?'

Elizabeth shook her head again, so Hélène resumed her lunch. The only sounds were the faint hum of bees going about their business in the flower border and an unseen robin giving vent to its melancholy song. Hélène seemed content to eat in silence, which Elizabeth found increasingly difficult to bear. At last she forced herself to speak. 'Did you come back to my apartment last night?' She phrased it as a question, although there was no doubt in her mind.

'Yes, of course; don't you remember? You were in rather a state. I heard you cry out even though I was in my office.'

'And you came up to my bedroom?' Elizabeth's brow furrowed in concentration.

'That's right. I had to use the spare key I keep in the office.' Hélène's tone was solicitous. 'You were very agitated. Something had upset you, a nightmare perhaps. Or maybe the kirsch; it's difficult to know.'

'I don't remember that at all,' muttered Elizabeth. 'But then you stayed to keep me company, is that right?'

'Yes, I didn't like to leave you in that state. It seemed the sensible thing to do. You soon calmed down and went back to sleep.'

Elizabeth considered these statements for a few moments but found them inconclusive. 'Did I wake up again, later in the night?'

It was Hélène's turn to pause before replying. 'Well, I'm not sure you were fully awake, but you did stir.'

'I don't remember much, but I'm sure …' Elizabeth looked skywards, turning her palms upwards in a gesture of confusion.

Hélène understood. 'I can see you're hazy about what happened. I'll try to put your mind at rest. Would you like me to do that?'

'Yes, please.' Elizabeth's voice was little more than a whisper

'You went back to sleep very quickly. So did I, as a matter of fact. But later – I don't know what time – you seemed to wake, or perhaps half wake would be more accurate.' Hélène paused, seemingly reluctant to continue.

'Go on,' prompted Elizabeth.

'Well, let's just say that you seemed to think I was your old school prefect flame.'

The import of Hélène's assertion took a moment or two to sink in. Elizabeth closed her eyes and put her head in her hands. 'Oh, for God's sake.'

Hélène resumed her solicitous role. 'Look, Elizabeth, it's

absolutely nothing to worry about. It was nothing new to me, as you know. In fact, I found it rather delightful, a reminder of my younger self. I should really thank you for it.' She adopted a sterner tone. 'But you have nothing to regret or reproach yourself for. It's one of life's experiences, and a pleasurable one at that. And of course it will be a secret known only to us, just as we have shared other secrets. Surely you can see that.'

'Yes, but … but what does it say about my marriage?'

'Your marriage is completely unaffected. You will carry on with your husband just as you always have.' Hélène was in full advisory mode. 'Every woman withholds secrets from her man, whether she realises it or not. It might be a character defect she dislikes, or that he's not a very good lover. We all do it, and you must do the same.'

'Well, I certainly have no intention of telling Bernard.'

'Good. What the eye doesn't see…' Hélène let the words hang in the air, favouring her companion with a reassuring smile. Elizabeth looked considerably less tense than when she had first appeared, and Hélène could detect no sign of panic or anger or even accusation. Bafflement appeared to be Elizabeth's principal emotion and Hélène was sure that would soon diminish to nothing. More importantly, her conscience did not appear too troubled, much reducing the risk of a damaging confession to her husband.

As Hélène gazed benevolently on a still-quiet Elizabeth, she felt a degree of satisfaction bordering on triumph. Notifying Gustave of her victory in the challenge – albeit with an undeclared adaptation – was a prospect she anticipated keenly.

❦

Chance brought about the meeting in the hall. A sudden shower sent Elizabeth and Bernard scurrying back to the house, just as it drove Gustave indoors from the courtyard.

Hélène heard the sound of their voices from her office but continued working.

Gustave and Bernard had only a passing acquaintance, not least because Bernard made no effort to cultivate friendship. Their relationship remained merely polite, usually a brief exchange about the weather. Nonetheless, Gustave knew that Bernard followed politics and international affairs, subjects that were close to his own heart. And, in view of the news, he determined to discover Bernard's opinion.

After a brief exchange about the downpour, Gustave broached his subject. 'I know you take an interest in such things, so may I ask what you think of the latest news, the agreement between Russia and Germany?'

Bernard recoiled slightly, as if struck by a minor blow. His eyes narrowed as he considered his reply. 'It's a disaster, a complete disaster. A non-aggression pact, the very thing Hitler needed to secure Germany's eastern border. You have to pity Poland.'

'Yes, quite so,' said Gustave, his concern obvious. 'Do you think the Germans will really invade Poland? After all, they have gained many territorial concessions already.'

'I am certain of it. And it will be soon.'

'Are you sure?' Gustave was unsettled by Bernard's certainty. 'With all due respect, how can you be so sure?'

'I have a number of customers in Germany, including a few who've become good friends. I phoned one of them yesterday, as soon as I heard the news. He lives in Berlin. He told me that German troops are already moving to the east in all kinds of transport, including civilian buses.' Bernard paused, suddenly concerned. 'He took a chance telling me that. It's the sort of thing that can get you arrested.'

Gustave's face grew longer. 'Surely they won't invade this year; after all, it is autumn already. Besides, both France and England have issued guarantees to the Poles. Surely that will be a deterrent?'

Bernard's only answer was a dismissive shake of the head. At that moment Hélène left her office; entering the hall she saw Gustave and Bernard standing temporarily silent, while a grave-faced Elizabeth stood a little apart.

'Why so gloomy? It's only a summer shower.'

'Monsieur Vermeulen thinks there will be war within weeks.'

Hélène's good spirits vanished in an instant. 'I'm sure Monsieur Vermeulen has his reasons, but surely that is too pessimistic.'

Bernard had little time for Hélène's doubts. 'No, Madame, I think you will find I am proved right. I have thought so for months, and nothing has changed my mind. Indeed, things have only got worse. This Russo–German pact is the last piece of Hitler's jigsaw.'

'But we have the new fortifications, the Maginot Line. Surely that will keep us safe?' Hélène's irritation bubbled to the surface. 'And if not, why on earth has the government spent all that money on it?'

Bernard did not rush to answer, so Gustave felt obliged to step in. 'The Line extends only as far as the Luxembourg border at Longwy. That's only a half hour's drive from here, as you know. But the fortifications will help, of course, if there's a conflict.'

'That's right, if there's a war.' Hélène's temper was rising, evident in her icy tone. 'I can't help feeling all this war talk is overdone. Pessimism helps nobody. What evidence is there that war is inevitable?'

'If Madame would open her eyes,' started Bernard, willing to pour petrol on the flames, 'she will see French army reservists being called up, troops deploying on the borders and air-raid shelters being built in Paris. These, I have to point out, are just the French preparations for war. They are nothing compared to Germany's.'

'I don't believe it. How would you know?'

Gustave tried a diplomatic intervention. 'Monsieur Vermeulen travels very widely throughout Europe, Hélène, and…'

But Hélène cared little for Gustave's diplomacy. 'And we are allied to the English, are we not? As allies, I seem to remember we won the last war. I don't imagine the Germans have forgotten that.'

'The British hardly have an army, Madame; they have a navy. Do you think they are going to sail their battleships up the Meuse to save France?'

Taken aback by Bernard's directness, Hélène could think of no immediate reply. An agitated Elizabeth pulled at Bernard's sleeve while Gustave could only mutter, 'Well, let us hope things work out for the best,' in the manner of a vacuous prayer.

But Bernard was not done. A dam had broken, and his frustrations now burst out. 'The trouble with the French is that they have no idea of their priorities. While they are captivated by holidays and a bicycle race, the Germans have re-armed and expanded Greater Germany without a shot being fired. And all the time it's been laid out in Hitler's book, in plain sight. "Mein Kampf" says it all, but the French have not understood.'

Hélène was sufficiently recovered to respond. 'And have you actually read this wretched book? Or are these stories something you have simply picked up from the alarmist press?' It was meant as a put-down but it misfired.

'I have read the book. Hitler is perfectly clear: he predicts one last gigantic battle with France, the outcome of which will determine Europe's future for generations.' Bernard could not resist adding, 'France will soon pay for its inattention.'

'That's rich, coming from a Belgian.' Hélène was also now in full flow. 'A cobbled-together country that doesn't even have a common language.'

'That may be so, Madame, but I understand you are from Alsace. Alsatians, of course, are more German than French, which explains much about your attitude.'

'That's enough!' shouted Elizabeth, seizing Bernard's arm. 'That's enough from both of you.'

'Quite so,' said Gustave, thoroughly alarmed. 'Please let us not fall out over events far beyond our control. I think it best if we conclude this conversation.'

He stepped into the space between Hélène and Bernard, while Elizabeth pulled her husband towards their apartment door. Nothing more was spoken.

❧

Having withdrawn to her apartment, Hélène's fury knew no bounds. She was not used to losing an argument but understood only too well that she had come off second best and been insulted into the bargain; insulted by a boorish, overbearing Belgian, and a Jew to boot. The Jewish element was pure conjecture but it suited Hélène to think that Bernard was Jewish. He was a businessman, after all, with the international connections typical of that race. And he was dark and intense, and dull and miserable and pessimistic…

New words failed her but, as her temper slowly subsided, the vacuum was filled by a desire for revenge. How familiar that feeling was to Hélène, a throwback to her early years in the town when many of the great and the good among its citizens had chosen to ignore, or even slight, their Alsatian newcomer with her jarring accent and the dubious political background of Alsace. Not that Hélène was in the least political; being Alsatian was sufficient to be condemned.

If her accent had long diminished to the barely perceptible, Hélène's capacity for revenge had certainly not. Not only was the feeling familiar but it sat comfortably with her. It was a character trait she had nurtured over the years, like a flawed infant now grown into a devious and malicious adult. So it was no surprise to Hélène when, out of her anger, there suddenly emerged a thought, a revenge so delightfully appealing that she laughed aloud at its prospect.

❧

The unfortunate exchange between Bernard and Hélène created an uncomfortable atmosphere in the house. Contact between the two had always been by chance, minimal and politely neutral, so this new tension was tolerable to them but their respective spouses were more affected. So, when Bernard Vermeulen resumed his travels a couple of days later with relations unrepaired, it was not certain whether something like normality would – or could – be resumed between the three people remaining.

It was Hélène who broke the ice. She sought out Elizabeth and apologised profusely. She was overwrought with all this talk of war, she said, and it had pushed her into an inexcusable argument which she deeply regretted. She hoped that Elizabeth and her husband could forgive her.

Elizabeth, acutely embarrassed by the affair, was glad to accept the apology. Although she did not say so, she had urged Bernard to apologise even though she thought Hélène had needlessly fuelled the argument. Bernard had only agreed to consider apologising and, to Elizabeth's chagrin, was still considering when he left on his latest travels. Now she felt Hélène's initiative left Bernard languishing on the moral low ground. An equally fulsome apology to Hélène would almost certainly restore peace but Elizabeth knew Bernard would find that difficult, if not impossible. However, if the prospect of good relations between Hélène and Bernard Vermeulen looked tentative at best, at least those with Hélène seemed fully restored.

❧

'By the way, I ought to mention something,' said Hélène, glancing up from her meal. Relations between the two women had revived sufficiently to resume their al fresco lunches under the cherry tree.

'Oh, really? What is it?' Elizabeth enquired.

'A minor problem has arisen, that's all. But you may be able to help.' She stopped speaking, as though expecting Elizabeth to divine an explanation.

'What sort of problem?'

'Can you recall the other night, the one when I was … concerned for you?' Hélène was studiously diplomatic in her choice of words.

'Yes, although I can't say I remember all that much, as you know.' Elizabeth's brow furrowed at the direction of the conversation. It was not an episode she felt entirely comfortable discussing.

'No, of course not; I understand completely.' Hélène exuded nothing but sympathy. 'No, this concerns the aftermath. You remember Amelie collected your bed linen the following day?'

Wondering at this line of enquiry, Elizabeth had to think for a moment. 'Yes, Amelie stripped the bed and took the laundry. Why, is something wrong?'

'It's just that she noticed something, a few hairs on the pillow slip. She can be quite sharp like that sometimes.' Hélène hesitated, as if reluctant to continue. 'She mentioned it to me, and that is my slight worry.'

'I'm not sure…' began Elizabeth, before tailing off with a questioning frown.

Hélène began again, more directly this time. 'You have blonde hair; your husband's is mid-brown but quite fine. Amelie is well aware of this, of course, since she sees you frequently. But she pointed out that a few hairs on your pillow were dark brown and thick. And she has drawn a conclusion, which she related to me with some relish, that you must have taken a lover.'

Elizabeth responded with growing concern, 'What on earth did you say?'

'Amelie is from typical peasant stock, born with a certain type of low intelligence that can be perceptive at times and very annoying. Of course, as her employer, I left her in no doubt that she should keep that information to herself. I can't be sure whether she realised the hair was mine. If she did, she was careful not to suggest it. However, my concern is that she may well gossip to her friends and, once out, the rumour will inevitably spread. That is of only marginal concern to me; my name is black enough already. But I would worry for you.'

Elizabeth's anxiety showed in her face. 'Do you really think she'll talk? After all, she would lose her job if you heard about it.' She paused for a moment before adding, 'Do you think I should pay her some money to keep quiet?'

'Certainly not; that would simply invite further problems. Where would it all end?' Hélène offered a thin smile of reassurance. 'As it happens, I have a solution. Amelie is beholden to Manien; I don't know all the details but other people's lives are invariably more complicated than appearances suggest. I do know he has considerable influence over her. I can ask Manien to have a word with our little peasant girl. I suspect he can be quite forceful if he chooses. With Manien on the one hand and my threat to her employment on the other, I think her silence can be reasonably assured.'

Elizabeth considered this solution with some reluctance. 'That sounds a little threatening but, if you think it will work, I suppose it's for the best. Do you think Manien will do as you ask? Won't you have to explain why you're asking?' She raised her hands to her face. 'Oh, this is so … awkward.'

'I can assure you he is the soul of discretion. In all my

dealings with Manien I have never known him divulge anything confidential. I'm sure he would be willing to help us. After all, he has helped you once before.'

Elizabeth's reply was fervent. 'I hope so. I really do. The last thing I want is some awful gossip spread about the town.'

'You mustn't worry. I will speak to Manien. I have every confidence in him.'

Hélène had good reason to be pleased. Chance had delivered an opportunity to exact retribution for a recent insult, and she had just initiated the process.

~

In recent days, Gustave's moods had oscillated even more than usual. Now, sitting in the comfortable surroundings of his modest library, he felt more at ease. There had been good news from the factory; at a board meeting that morning, Hunblot had announced that an unexpected enquiry had been received. It concerned their company's willingness and ability to produce military equipment such as mess tins and water bottles. A competitor business in Rheims could not cope with all the work and needed to subcontract. The prospect of secure and long-lasting work for the factory was excellent news, even if it required an initial cost in changing the presses. And, since Gustave received the bulk of his meagre remuneration in dividends, any boost to profitability would be most welcome.

The news helped offset his concern over the recent unpleasantness between Hélène and Bernard Vermeulen. Fortunately, his relations with Elizabeth seemed unaffected, although both expressed their deep regret about what had occurred. At their one short meeting since the disagreement, the row between their respective spouses had been the main talking point, although Elizabeth had also given Gustave her latest piece of writing. And it was to this that Gustave now gave his attention.

It was a longer manuscript than anything Elizabeth had produced before. Even so, Gustave had read it twice already. Now he read it for a third time, the better to consider its merits. There was no doubt that her writing had improved: this story was better structured and progressed with a more satisfactory flow. Sentence and paragraph construction were also improved, as was the use of similes. But while these technical elements registered with Gustave, it was the storyline that stole his attention.

Previously, Elizabeth's short stories had deployed romantic plots in which a chaste heroine and a dashing suitor eventually came together after overcoming some comparatively minor difficulty. This story was quite different. The principal character was a young woman married to worthy husband working in the diplomatic corps. A war-threatening crisis required the husband's frequent absences, during which time the wife became the focus of a handsome serial seducer. Although initially repelled by his reputation, her resistance was gradually eroded by her husband's unavoidable neglect. She became increasingly curious about the charming libertine, until curiosity became desire. Only the last-minute resolution of the diplomatic crisis and the return of her husband saved the weakening heroine from a fateful surrender.

It was clear to Gustave that the story was influenced by Elizabeth's reading. Aspects of Emma Bovary were present; the villain probably derived from the scheming Vicomte de Valmont of *Les Liaisons dangereuses*. But whatever Elizabeth's inspiration, Gustave wondered whether the story revealed a change in her own attitude, for there was more than an echo of her own circumstances. Perhaps wearying of loneliness, she had become more susceptible to the attractions of others.

Gustave pondered this possibility with acute interest.

Although Elizabeth had always displayed considerable affection towards him, there had been no hint of anything more. Now it seemed possible that circumstances had changed and an opportunity might be present, if he was bold enough to pursue it.

༄

Hélène came as the bearer of good news. Its importance was such that she couldn't wait until the following day, so she hastened to Elizabeth's door despite the lateness of the hour. Her smile conveyed suppressed excitement. 'I have something to tell you,' she said, stepping uninvited across the threshold.

Only when they were seated in the living room did Hélène begin to explain. 'I have just been speaking to Manien.' Even now she avoided coming directly to the point. 'I explained that what I had to say was highly confidential and that I trusted him to keep it so. He readily agreed – we are long-time confidants – but I could see he was intrigued.'

Hélène paused, whether for effect or to choose her words was impossible to say. Elizabeth's look betrayed a degree of impatience. Hélène continued, 'I told him what had happened, that you drank more than usual and I became concerned for you. And that Amelie noticed different hair on your pillow and was speculating about a lover. He listened carefully, particularly when I mentioned my concern about potential gossip. He agrees that Amelie is almost certain to talk eventually.'

'And…' said Elizabeth, a shade sharply.

'Quite spontaneously, he offered to help. Manien understands our difficulty. He's going to speak to Amelie this evening, if he can. He is concerned that she might talk sooner rather than later. He'll find out whether the wretched girl has already blabbed, although he thinks it unlikely.' Hélène drew a deep breath. 'I tell you, Elizabeth, Manien is a man in a thousand.'

'Well, it's certainly a relief, I know that.' Elizabeth reflected for a moment. 'It's good of him to help, but it's also thanks to you.'

'Nonsense; we're both equally involved. Manien is doing us both a favour.' Once again Hélène paused before continuing. 'As I say, it was a spontaneous offer of help but, as he departed, Manien did make a request. He asked if he might be introduced to you.'

'What?' exclaimed Elizabeth, taken aback. 'Whatever made him ask that?'

'I think he's just curious. I've told him you write, as well as immersing yourself in French literature, and he finds that intriguing. Manien is largely self-taught and continues to try and improve himself. I admire him for it and I'm sure you will, too. He doesn't pretend to be an intellectual – which I also admire – but he's a man of surprisingly broad interests.'

'I see.' Elizabeth took a moment to absorb this information. 'I don't know, Hélène; I'm not sure it's … sensible, if you understand me. I don't want to avoid being the subject of gossip about one topic only to start being the subject of another. I'm sure he's perfectly well-meaning but…'

'I'm surprised you think either Manien or I would be so crass as to allow anything regrettable to happen. No, I will make sure it is perfectly discreet.' Hélène seemed to have assumed Elizabeth would agree with her plan.

'I'm not at all sure, Hélène. I mean, would you be there as well? And where do think such a meeting could take place. It couldn't possibly be here.'

'Of course I can be present, if that's what you want. Manien does some business in Metz, so Cecile's would be the ideal place. Either the bar or the café would be suitable, away from this town's prying eyes.'

Elizabeth was not convinced. 'I don't know, Hélène. Meeting at Cecile's seems a bit much.' She chose not to mention the nature of the secondary business conducted at Cecile's.

Hélène allowed her frustration to show. 'Really, Elizabeth, you're acting like some shrinking violet. The man is doing you a considerable favour, and you seem to be cavilling at some minor request. I understand your concern but it is baseless. And please remember I have your interests in mind. We're friends, aren't we?'

'Yes. I'm sorry, Hélène, of course we are.' Elizabeth managed a thin smile. 'It's just a surprise that's all, and a little conspiratorial. I certainly wouldn't want Bernard to find out.'

'It's perfectly harmless, Elizabeth. Think of your walks with Xavier. Pleasant strolls around Metz with a charming companion; informative, as well as fun. Very sensibly, you said nothing about them to your husband. View a meeting with Manien in the same light, but even more interesting.'

This reminder of Xavier prompted a defensive reply from Elizabeth. 'My walks around Metz are different. Xavier is nothing more than a guide, just like he would be for any tourist.'

'Yes, that's true up – to a point. But you must be aware by now why Xavier is so often found at Cecile's and why he has no obvious employment. It's because certain well-bred ladies seek his company. To put it bluntly, Elizabeth, he is a gigolo. I cannot believe this information comes as a surprise to you.'

'Not entirely, no, although it's rather disconcerting to have it confirmed. And, knowing that, I wonder why you put me in his company.'

'Because it's perfectly harmless, that's why. While Cecile and I talk business, it's surely better for you to see Metz in good company of your own age.' Hélène's glance hardened.

'When you suspected the truth about Xavier, you could easily have stopped the arrangement but you didn't. Why not? Because you enjoy his company and it harms nobody. Meeting Manien will be no different.'

Elizabeth did not reply. Hélène's arguments were difficult to refute since they were largely true. She was well aware her association with Xavier could be misinterpreted, even if her behaviour was blameless. The visits to Cecile's premises, housing a confidential business above a legitimate one, could be misconstrued. Fortunately, Metz was well away from the town and there had been no hint of damaging repercussions.

Despite her misgivings, Elizabeth found it difficult to refuse. 'All right, Hélène. I suppose there's no harm in meeting Manien – should I call him that? – as a thank you for his help. And to please you, since you seem so set on it.'

Hélène's features relaxed into a smile of satisfaction. 'Good. Everything will be fine. And you have saved me from embarrassment, since I told Manien I was sure you would agree.' Seizing the moment, she added, 'We could go to Metz tomorrow.'

'No, that's not possible. Bernard is due home this evening.'

'When does he leave again?'

'I'm not sure. He's going to one of the factories in England in Luton, just outside London.' Elizabeth had no idea why she volunteered this superfluous information. 'I'll have to let you know.'

'Very well, but make it as soon as possible.' Hélène seemed irritated by any prospect of delay. 'I wouldn't want to keep Manien waiting too long.'

֍

As expected, Bernard Vermeulen returned to the apartment. Hélène saw husband and wife out together on successive days, although she deliberately avoided meeting them. On the morning of the third day, Hélène noticed that the station wagon had gone but of Elizabeth there was no sign. She did not show up for their shared visits to the market or the al fresco lunches. There were no chance meetings in the hall or the garden. As Elizabeth remained conspicuous by her absence, Hélène grew increasingly impatient.

The news of the German invasion of Poland registered even with Hélène. While Gustave fulminated about the catastrophic failure of diplomacy, she considered possible consequences closer to home, not least to their hard-won financial security. But it also added urgency to a particular outstanding matter.

꙳

The knock on the door surprised Elizabeth only because of the lateness of the hour. She had suspected that her avoidance of Hélène would probably provoke an enquiry at some stage, but this was rather later in the day than she had expected. Sure enough, on opening the door she found Hélène waiting close to the threshold. There was a faint smile on her aquiline face, but it radiated little warmth.

'Ah, you are here, after all. I'd begun to think you'd left without telling me,' Hélène said.

'No, it's nothing like that; it's just that I've been busy,' replied Elizabeth, at the same time deciding to disclose the unwelcome news. 'You probably realise we'll be moving on soon, in view of the political situation. Bernard is away making arrangements while I've been busy tidying up things here.' It was the excuse she had decided upon earlier.

'Of course, I understand completely. After all, you told me as much a while ago.' Hélène's smile deepened a fraction. 'May I come in?'

'Yes, of course.'

They made their way to the living room, where Hélène immediately spoke. 'It's such a shame you are leaving so soon but it's good to hear that you are tidying up loose ends. With that in mind, I'm able to help you.'

'Oh,' said Elizabeth, mildly curious. 'In what way?'

'I've arranged for you to keep your word.'

'Keep my…' Elizabeth stopped, perplexed

'Yes,' said Hélène, her voice suddenly more hard edged. 'Surely you remember? You promised to return a favour with a favour. You promised to meet Manien.'

Disconcerted, Elizabeth hardly knew what to say. 'Surely things have changed, Hélène; you must see that. I thought it was just a suggestion, something we might do if it were convenient to both of us. But now I'm busy preparing to leave, I can't imagine I'm going to find the time…'

'On the contrary,' interrupted Hélène, 'that's why I'm here now, to help you make the time and keep your promise. A promise, you remember, that you made not just to Manien but also to me.' She inclined her head, suddenly mischievous. 'As for making the time, there is no time like the present. Manien will be here any minute now.'

Elizabeth was open mouthed in disbelief. 'You can't mean it, Hélène. Please tell me you're joking.'

'Don't be difficult, Elizabeth. It's perfectly discreet. Nobody will be any the wiser. Besides, I'm here to keep you company.'

'But Bernard is on his way back from England! What if he finds Manien here?' This was a white lie; he was due back late the following day.

'Then we must make sure Manien doesn't overstay his welcome.'

'I don't like it, Hélène. What if I simply don't answer the door?'

'I can't believe you would be so rude. What sort of response is that to someone who's helped you in a not insignificant matter? Please don't be awkward. It's just a social visit; I expect it will be over in half an hour.'

Elizabeth suddenly had a thought. 'I know Manien helped me by speaking to Amelie. I understand that and I'm grateful. But I'll be gone in a few days so it hardly matters what she says about me then, does it? I'll be far beyond the reach of small-town gossip.'

'Listen to yourself, Elizabeth. You're beginning to sound small minded and mean. You haven't left yet, and Manien is a very particular man. I don't know what he might do if he felt slighted.'

'Surely you're not suggesting he would say anything to Bernard, are you?' Elizabeth hesitated, dismayed by the possibility. 'I didn't think he was…'

She stopped speaking, interrupted by a knock at the door.

'Leave it to me,' said Hélène, rising to her feet. Before Elizabeth could object, she was gone; there came the sounds of a door opening and brief, muted speech. A few moments later Hélène returned, closely followed by Manien. He was just as Elizabeth remembered him: a stocky, powerful figure with a pleasant, open face devoid of any hint of guile. But it was his eyes that dominated. Once again, Elizabeth noted their deep, encompassing liquidity, well-aware they were studying her. Instinctive politeness made her rise to be introduced.

'Elizabeth, this is Manien. He has been dying to be introduced to you.' Having made the formal introduction, Hélène sat down. Manien acknowledged the introduction with a brief nod towards Elizabeth while Hélène, the mistress of ceremonies, invited him to sit down. She continued by suggesting that Elizabeth produce a bottle of wine and some glasses.

Only when this had been done did Manien speak. 'I understand you write for a hobby.' His voice was a shade deeper than Bernard's.

'Yes, but not very well.'

'And what do you like to write?'

Elizabeth was sitting very straight and prim. 'Just short stories and a few poems; they're really not very good.'

'I believe Monsieur de Bresson encourages you.'

'Yes, he's been very helpful.'

'Elizabeth is being modest,' Hélène interjected. 'Gustave says her writing is very much improved. He says her latest story was easily her best yet; perceptive as well as dramatic.'

Conversation remained stilted on Elizabeth's part; she spoke little more than politeness required. But Hélène was not content to let things drift. With some skill she kept the conversation going, persevering in the manner of a determined matchmaker. Although Elizabeth relaxed to some degree, it was apparent that she was less than comfortable. It remained a conversation largely conducted by Hélène and Manien, with brief contributions from Elizabeth in response to questions.

Then, after half an hour, Hélène suddenly stood up. 'I must go; Gustave will be wondering where I am.' Without waiting for a response, she said good night and walked swiftly to the apartment door.

Elizabeth caught up with her as she stepped through the doorway. 'You can't leave me alone with him.' Her voice was quiet but strained.

Hélène was unrepentant. 'You'll be fine.'

'How do you know?'

'Because I've been alone with him many times.'

'That's different.'

'No, it's not.' Hélène was impatient to go.

'But how will he leave the house when it's locked up?'

'Manien knows the way.' She smiled thinly at Elizabeth.

'Just be natural and you'll be fine. Make the most of this opportunity.' With this enigmatic injunction, she turned on her heels and walked off, her footsteps echoing softly across the hall.

Elizabeth watched her go then turned back into the apartment.

Manien was still sitting in the living room. Seeing Elizabeth hesitating in the doorway, he felt obliged to speak. 'That was an abrupt departure.'

'Yes,' Elizabeth said, still angry. 'Is that how it was planned?'

'Certainly not by me or with my knowledge. But then Madame de Bresson is a law unto herself. She's very intelligent but works in mysterious ways.' Manien paused for a moment before adding, 'Won't you come and sit down? You're making me nervous.'

The irony was not lost on Elizabeth, who gave a wry smile, but the remark was well-judged because it prompted her to resume her seat. 'I'm not sure where I stand with Hélène. She's been a good friend, really very good to me, but this…' She displayed her bafflement with a shrug of her shoulders and upturned hands.

'Understandably so. She assured me you had requested a meeting, so it would seem we've both been managed to some degree. But that is Madame de Bresson's way, although it sometimes misfires.'

'Are you saying this meeting was not your idea in return for speaking to Amelie?'

Manien shook his head. 'No, not quite that. It's true that I expressed an interest in meeting you, but hardly like this. I can see you are upset. That's not how people should meet. It was much better when I mended your puncture.'

'Ah, yes, you were very kind. I believe I interrupted your fishing.'

'It was of no consequence. I spend more than enough

time fishing; it was my pleasure to help a lady in distress.'

'Well, I was very grateful. It's still holding up, incidentally, your puncture repair. You did a very good job.' Elizabeth suddenly realised much of her anxiety seemed to have departed with Hélène. She decided to be straightforward. 'Hélène was right that I've been avoiding her. You've probably realised I wasn't looking forward to this meeting. But I am very grateful for your help with Amelie. It's just that I felt Hélène was being too overbearing.'

Manien nodded sympathetically. 'Of course; she will never make a diplomat or anything like that. I hope her clumsiness has not done any permanent damage.'

'Only if we let it.' Elizabeth suddenly felt relieved and oddly liberated. 'As you say, Hélène appears to have manipulated us both. That being so, perhaps we should drink to our absent friend who has done so much to bring about our meeting. None of that ordinary wine for me, either – I'm going to have a kirsch. Would you like a glass?'

And so their conversation slipped into naturalness. Manien was quietly attentive, asking straightforward questions about her writing and the books she had read, questions that encouraged easy replies. As he absorbed every word, Elizabeth responded with growing confidence as her natural temperament reasserted itself. Under Manien's unstinting attention, she rather lost track of time. Even had she been aware, it became increasingly doubtful whether she would have minded.

In fact, after a swift glance at his watch, it was Manien who mentioned the time. 'It seems to be quite late. I really ought to be going.'

Lounging on the sofa, Elizabeth consulted the mantel clock. 'Oh, is that the time? Well, perhaps you're right. I'll see you to the door.'

She uncoiled from the sofa and stood up. Neither spoke as she led the way into the dimly lit hall and past the stairs.

In the restricted space by door, she turned and faced Manien. He stepped into the narrow gap between them, took her in his arms and kissed her on the mouth, just as she had expected, and wanted.

※

The British declaration of war crushed Gustave's last desperate hopes of a diplomatic resolution to the crisis. When the French government followed suit a few hours later, Gustave heard the news while gathered with Hunblot and others friends at the Station Hotel. The atmosphere was one of resigned gloom, intensified by a false report of an air raid on Paris.

He left for home soon after six. It was still warm, for it had been a perfect late summer's day. But, for a Sunday, the town was unusually busy. The military traffic was to be expected but Gustave's attention was drawn to the number of civilian cars. These were heavily loaded, baggage crammed into the interiors to the extent that any passengers were scarcely visible. More bags and boxes were tied to the roofs, sometimes untidily as though packed in a hurry. A mattress topped the roof of one car and Gustave wondered whether it was meant to protect against air attack. He guessed these civilian vehicles were leaving the area for they were all going in one direction, away from the border.

Arriving back at the house, he found Hélène in their living room. His return seemed to rouse her from a kind of reverie, unusual for a woman so little given to introspection. Gustave assumed she had not listened to the news. 'In case you haven't heard, I'm afraid it's the worst possible news.' He avoided the word 'war' as he guessed its likely incendiary effect. Hélène gave him her attention, as if awaiting a briefing, but did not speak.

'The government has announced the evacuation of

Strasburg and all the territory between the Maginot Line and the German border. I've seen several civilian cars already, loaded with belongings, heading for Paris or anywhere else away from the border. Hunblot thinks there may well be a mass movement, even from centres like Metz.'

'Why would people do that? Are we not protected by the fortifications? And don't we still have our own army and air force?'

'It's the memory of the last war, Hélène. You know how this area suffered: Cantigny, St Mihiel, Verdun, for heaven's sake. The Germans occupied large parts of this region for virtually the whole of the war. You can't wonder at people opting for something safer.' Gustave hesitated before adding, 'Hunblot is concerned that the Germans could bypass the Maginot Line by coming through Luxembourg and Belgium.'

Hélène's face distorted with frustration. 'For pity's sake, Gustave, don't you have a mind of your own? Hunblot says this; Hunblot thinks that; Hunblot believes the other. Why do you always treat that dreadful old poseur like some sort of messiah?'

'Well, he was a captain on the General Staff in the last war,' muttered Gustave. It sounded lame even to him.

'I'm amazed the government hasn't begged him to sort out this mess. Then we'd all be able to sleep safely in our beds at night.'

There was brief a hiatus until Gustave ventured, 'Whatever faith we place in the Maginot Line, we are still vulnerable here. People are beginning to leave and I think we should do the same. I've a cousin near Toulouse; I'm sure we could go down there.'

'Have you gone mad? Are you really suggesting we run away even before a shot has been fired?' Hélène's frustration lurched into anger. 'Don't you realise our living is here?

Everything we've worked for is in this town. What good is Toulouse to us? How do you expect to make a living there? Or are you expecting to live on your cousin's charity?'

'No, of course not. But we have some savings, or we could sell one, or even both, of our other properties. We are not without assets.'

Her face flushed with anger, Hélène barely controlled her temper. 'I have spent years reversing the financial mess I inherited when I married you. Now, just as it's giving us some reward, you want us to give it all up. Have you learnt nothing about economics at that wretched factory? If people really are running away, there will be no buyers. Unless, of course, we practically give our properties away. There are always speculators.'

Gustave was tempted to respond 'just like you', but decided against it. Instead, he pursued his original idea. 'I'm going to contact my cousin. You seem to have no alternative proposal.'

'Enquire all you like but, contrary to what you think, I did hear the news. I understand circumstances are changing and that it will affect us. The Vermeulens could leave any day now that war is declared. The Cartelets have a son in Rennes so they could go there, but they are surely too old to think of moving. It's possible one of the other tenants may go but I doubt both.' Hélène paused, choosing her words with care, for there were aspects of their finances she would not divulge to Gustave. 'But with all this uncertainty, I have made one change already: Amelie is finished.'

'What!' exclaimed Gustave. 'Without even consulting me? That's very harsh, Hélène.'

'I'm not at all sorry. She was insolent recently, not for the first time. And she had the nerve to ask for a month's wages even though she didn't want to work out her notice. I paid her for one week – some would say she was lucky to get that.'

'As ever, generous to a fault,' murmured Gustave, more to himself than Hélène. He was sorry Amelie was gone; there had been some flirtatious moments between them, although the prospect of Hélène's wrath had quickly doused any thoughts of passion. He reverted to more pressing matters. 'You are missing the point. Yes, we may survive on a reduced income, but what is the point if an air attack reduces the town to rubble, like Guernica? Or if the Germans breach or bypass the fortifications and this area becomes a battleground again? What if they actually manage to take back Alsace and Lorraine? What would we do then, even supposing we survive?'

Hélène had heard enough of this pessimistic theorising. 'I would let the properties to the Germans. They would need accommodation and might even be better payers.'

'Ah, there speaks a true Alsatian. All you need to do is brush up on your German and you'll be perfectly placed.'

'It's the language of my childhood, Gustave. I won't need much practice.'

Gustave's felt his temper being tested. 'I'm beginning to wonder where your loyalties lie, Hélène. You should be careful before speaking like that or people may begin to doubt your French credentials.'

Hélène snorted her derision. 'In case you have forgotten, when I returned home after the war I found many of my friends being forcibly expelled to Germany. Expelled from France by the French, Gustave. Yes, some were settlers but they had lived in Alsace for forty years. My friends were born there and knew no other home, but they were bundled off to Germany just the same. They lost everything – houses, friends, businesses, all left behind. You may wonder all you like about my "Frenchness" but my attitude simply reflects what I have experienced over the years. France is a very mixed bag for me.'

Gustave was not inclined to argue further. 'I refuse to get bogged down in the rights and wrongs of history. We are where we are, and that is dangerously close to the frontier of two nations now at war. You are naïve to the point of foolishness if you don't understand that.' He avoided saying 'stupidity', but in a rare moment of assertiveness continued, 'I insist that we begin making preparations to leave.'

Her temper now under control, Hélène studied her husband with cool detachment. 'If you insist we leave, Gustave, then it will be the parting of the ways. I will not leave this house. I will not abandon everything I have worked for. You have shown little enough interest in our finances over the years, so your grasp of them is, let's say, somewhat incomplete. They are stronger than you realise. If I leave, everything will collapse and I will not let that happen.'

'As usual, Hélène, you are the mistress of opacity. But even if I'm not responsible for every last sou that comes into this house, I do understand the danger we are in. What use are our properties if they are bombed to oblivion and us with them? Have it your own way; you usually do. But I will be contacting my cousin and making my own arrangements.' Gustave took a deep breath, as though relieved he had made a decision. And then a random thought occurred to him. 'A pity. If the Vermeulens leave, we shall never conclude our challenge.'

'What?' Momentarily thrown by the change of subject, Hélène quickly recovered. 'I can hardly believe what I'm hearing. Is that really a priority with you? But, since you've raised the subject, I can tell you that it has been concluded and you lost again.'

Gustave stared at his wife. 'I don't believe you.'

'Well, you should. And I adapted the rules a little, just to make it more interesting.'

'What do you mean?'

'I bedded your precious Elizabeth, that's what I mean.'

'Liar!' Gustave choked with rage. 'You're making it up to spite me.'

'Not at all, Gustave. Surely you didn't think I could bring myself to pursue that ghastly husband, did you? No, I decided on a far more pleasurable option.'

Gustave's stunned silence prompted Hélène to turn the screw. 'It wasn't very difficult. She's a spirited girl, with just the sort of curiosity to tempt her into pastures new. And I don't know why you should be surprised at me. I seem to remember you persuaded me into bed with a woman when I was hardly more than your blushing bride.'

'Your spite knows no bounds, Hélène,' muttered Gustave, recovering the power of speech. 'You have become a truly hateful and perverted woman, a rival to Lucrezia Borgia. God knows what poison runs through your veins. How could you treat Elizabeth so?'

'Don't be so high and mighty with me. You instigated the challenge, remember, just as you always have. What was so different this time? Or is it that you've fallen in love with the girl, as you usually do.'

'She deserved better from you, her supposed friend,' shouted Gustave.

'Oh, don't be so precious about your beloved Elizabeth. Let me tell you something else, something I'm surprised you haven't discovered for yourself. She is a woman of very diverse tastes. And it took Manien to satisfy them.'

'Never!' Gustave's face distorted with rage. 'Liar. Bitch!'

'You should have been there, Gustave. How she writhed and squirmed under his attentions. I could hear them from downstairs – and all in the marital bed.'

'Shut up! It's a despicable lie and I won't hear any more.'

'She was only curious about him at the beginning but we know where curiosity can lead, don't we? After all, we've been there ourselves. Elizabeth's curiosity kept growing and growing until eventually it became a fateful desire. I didn't try to dissuade her, it's true, but why should I? I'm not her keeper. In fact, I arranged their meeting; a tryst, I imagine you would call it, Gustave.'

But Gustave was beyond listening. Apoplectic with rage, he suddenly turned and stumbled from the room.

Feeling a little unsteady, Hélène sat down. She was surprised to notice that her hands were shaking, an almost imperceptible tremor to the tips of her fingers. The implications of their row began to sink in. It was always the same: the certainty that she could best Gustave in an argument encouraged her to exaggerate to further underscore his weakness. Now she wondered whether she had overdone it, just to wound Gustave further.

Hélène's desire for revenge had willed that Manien take the Belgian's wife. She had done all she could to bring that about, but Manien had assured her that nothing had passed, an inexplicable, infuriating failure of her plan. Then anger with Gustave had spawned a fiction to score a point. But scoring points was one thing, humiliation another. If their row had followed the usual pattern, some sort of reconciliation or compromise would surely have been possible. Now Hélène wasn't so sure, for she had never seen him so affected.

༒

Darkness was falling as Bernard Vermeulen reached the town. He was tired. An early start, the ferry crossing and a long drive had all contributed to his weariness; it was compounded by nagging sense of anxiety, for it was the appalling news that had brought him hurrying back to France.

The station-wagon headlights partially illuminated the narrow streets, picking out occasional, indistinct pedestrians as he drove. At last he reached the house and carefully manoeuvred the clumsy vehicle through the narrow gateway into the yard. He parked the station wagon and switched off the engine and headlights. The sudden silence and darkness caused him to sit for a moment, grateful that the journey was over.

Opening the car door he climbed out, his limbs stiff after hours at the wheel. From among the boxes in the rear he pulled out his suitcase, closed the door and locked it. He started to walk to his apartment but had taken only a few steps when he became aware of a figure emerging from the shadows of the stable building.

'Monsieur Vermeulen,' said Amelie. 'May I speak with you?'

～

Gustave slept badly, continually disturbed by the hateful images that overwhelmed his brain and refused to fade. Eventually, as dawn broke, he heard a vehicle in the street, a welcome distraction from his obsessive thoughts. It stopped in front of the house and the engine died. The sound of a car door being opened was sufficient to draw Gustave out of bed and he shuffled over to the window. Through a gap in the ill-fitting shutters, he saw that it was the Vermeulen's station wagon.

As he puzzled over the cause of such early activity, he heard the front door slam shut. Two figures came into view. Elizabeth Vermeulen, head bowed and strangely hesitant, walked to the car and climbed in. Bernard Vermeulen opened the station-wagon's rear doors and pushed two suitcases into the vehicle with shocking carelessness before going to the driver's door. As he made to enter the vehicle he suddenly stopped. Looking up at the house, he shouted, 'Salaud!' and shook his fist with such venom that Gustave drew back from the window. Seconds later, the engine started and the station wagon drew away.

~

It was nearly mid-day before Hélène de Bresson's body was found. It lay in a neighbour's shed, a few metres beyond the de Bressons' boundary. The initial police examination of the body found two severe head wounds which, although certainly disabling, left some doubt whether they were actually fatal. They thought she had been dead for about twelve hours and that she had almost certainly first been attacked elsewhere.

An apparently distraught Gustave struggled to give a comprehensible account of the previous evening, although he was scrupulously careful to attribute their row solely to the proposed move to Toulouse. Providing the names of people with access to the house came more easily.

Amelie provided the police with a studied character assassination of Hélène but, oddly, omitted any mention of her final conversation with Bernard Vermeulen. Manien was interviewed late that afternoon. He had a strong alibi for the previous evening until about ten o'clock when he had returned to his house. Since he lived alone, there was no one to corroborate his assertion that he had remained there for the rest of the night. Of equal interest to the police was the departure of the Vermeulens, although Gustave was at a loss to know where they might have gone. The list of possible suspects was further complicated by the presence on the edge of town of a regiment of Algerian Zouaves, some of whom had broken their confinement to camp and committed a series of thefts from properties.

The following day it became apparent that Manien had disappeared. During the same day, having failed to find a key to Hélène's small wall safe, the police called in a locksmith. When opened, it contained an accounts book, immaculately written up in Hélène's hand. It listed the names and payments – ostensibly for insurance – made by a number of well-to-do ladies of the town. Each individual was allocated a separate envelope in which were indelicate photographs, their poor quality and composition indicating they were taken without the subject's knowledge. A Minox miniature camera was also lodged in the safe.

Hélène's business-like revenge on the town's bourgeoisie had suddenly provided a number of additional motives for murder, as Manien well knew.

Appalled at the prospect of a widespread scandal, the mayor used all his influence to limit the police investigation. It was convenient that Manien, the suspect about whom there were such unwholesome rumours, had disappeared, perhaps to his old haunts in Marseille or even North Africa.

After its initial activity, the police investigation quickly lost impetus, amounting to little more than going through the motions. In the absence of an arrest and trial, detailed evidence remained withheld from the public domain, limiting the scandal to salacious speculation. For months Hélène de Bresson's murder remained a persistent, if slowly declining, topic of conversation until, one perfect May day, it was finally consigned to oblivion by the German blitzkrieg machine.

Lightning Source UK Ltd.
Milton Keynes UK
UKHW021512070519
342241UK00006BA/512/P